# Midsummer Dreams

### Ian Riddle

Michael Terence Publishing

First published in paperback by
Michael Terence Publishing in 2020
www.mtp.agency




ISBN 9781913289829





Cover image
Copyright © Ian & Annita Riddle
From the original watercolour,
'Lansallos Street, Polperro, Cornwall' by Hazel Moore


Cover design
Copyright © 2020 Michael Terence Publishing

*They said, 'Do Different'*

# Contents

# *List of Players*

All the world's a stage,
And all the men and women merely players;
They have their exits and their entrances.

*(Jacques - As You Like It, Act II, Scene VII, William Shakespeare)*

————————

| | |
|---|---|
| The Tour Guide | Narrator |
| Butcher Trelawney | Former Butcher, now dead |
| The Butcher's Wife | Also dead |
| Tamsyn | Daughter of the above, very much alive |
| Jack | Tamsyn's husband and now Butcher |
| Johnny Polmayne | Could-be Artist & Self-confessed Wastrel |
| Abi Polmayne | His long-suffering wife |
| Molly Pendarritt | Primary School Head Teacher & Hopeless Romantic |

| April & May Nancarrow | Twin sisters and spinsters; Bakers to the village. |
| 'Old' Bill Pascoe | General Handyman to the sisters. |
| | |
| The Captain | Joint owner, with his wife, of the restaurant, 'The Captain's Table' |
| The Captain's Wife | |
| | |
| Louise | Young widow, owner of Rose Cottage, a local B&B |
| | |
| Elizabeth Trevail (Lizzy) | Single mother |
| Two Little People | Lizzy's offspring |
| Lizzy's Mother | |
| | |
| Jason Henley | The Pie and Pasty Maker |
| Sarah Henley (née Pendragon) | |
| | His wife |
| | |
| Tom Penhale | Retired Fisherman and long-time Widower |
| | |
| Bob & Betty Braintree | Proprietors of the 'Cornish Crafts' Gift shop |
| | |
| Allan & Jenifer MacDonald | |
| | Proprietors of 'The Saucy Cod' Fish and Chip shop |

| Joan & Henry | Semi-retired; proprietors of 'The Fudge Shop' |
| Rockabilly Joe | Former Rock Star, now semi-recluse. A scarecrow of a man |
| Rose | Fan & Fantasist of Rockabilly and his music |

<u>Assorted shop owners</u>:

Patience

Duncan Thomas

John & Anne Tregear

The Trendy Young Couple

<u>Featuring</u>:

| Bastet, the cat | Also known as 'The Cat', owner of Treddoch Harbour (in her feline mind), ancient Egyptian Goddess, reincarnate, (in the mind of her owner, Molly) |

# Advertisement

## GUIDED TOUR OF CORNWALL

### The Land of Mystery and Magic

Don't miss this unique opportunity to sample the delights and wonders of England's most mysterious county, **Cornwall**. Cornwall, a land where for centuries, magic and reality have collided, mixed and mingled, a land where fact and fiction intertwine until the lines so blur, they go beyond mortal understanding.

Cornwall, the land of Camelot, of Arthur, its Once and Future King and of Guinevere his Queen. Cornwall, the land of diminutive Piskies and great Giants. The land of The Hurlers, the remnants of a group of men turned to stone for playing games on a Sunday! And, who knows, we may even catch a glimpse the Beast of Bodmin Moor as we pass.

Book your place now on this week-long tour, including a special **one-day trip to Treddoch Harbour,** a traditional Cornish fishing village, under the supervision of your own personal tour guide. Treddoch Harbour, a village steeped in history, where little seems to have changed over the centuries.

As a bonus, there's even an opportunity for you to meet with some of the locals and lunch in an olde worlde restaurant on the quayside, **'The Captain's Table'.**
All's included in the price.

Be sure to book your place quickly, spaces are limited.

**WELCOME TO CORNWALL - LAND OF LEGEND**

# By Way of an Introduction

*By Tre, Pol and Pen*
*Shall ye know all Cornishmen[1]*
(anon)

It's Midsummer in Treddoch Harbour, the time of the year when daylight seems to want to run on forever and night is just an unwanted and unwarranted intrusion.

It's that time of year when the blackbird can still be heard singing far into the evening and children are resentful of going to bed, for daylight, somehow, manages to worm its way through even the tightest of drawn curtains.

Grown-ups too are tempted to stay awake just that little bit longer, even though they know they shouldn't; work lurks behind the coming morning's alarm. Sitting out of doors though in the soft, warm air with a glass of something or other is always a preferable alternative. Winter, with its sharp nights and damp days, will come and confine them soon enough they know.

Not only is this Midsummer in general, but today, by chance, as we visit Treddoch Harbour, that sea-skirted, salt-washed, seagull-pooped-on community that lies snuggle-safe between its cliffs on Cornwall's southern coast, towards the eastern end it is, more specifically, June the twenty-first, Midsummer's Day, the Summer's Solstice.

---

1 Also Nancarrow, Jago and Enys

Today is that singular day of days in the calendar when the morning light comes streaming so early that it might seem to the untutored mind, that the hour's much later in fact than it is. It's especially true today, for the sky's clear, the weather's forecast to be more than fair and the temperatures are already on the rise, keeping pace with the ascending sun.

The blackbird has barely slept.

As special as Midsummer's Day might be in some quarters though, the Solstice isn't greeted to any particular degree here, not in Treddoch. It's certainly not hailed in any Henge-like fashion that's for sure. There's most definitely no one hanging around with specific intent to do a meet and greet and shout with cheery enthusiasm as the sun pops its head over the rim of the horizon.

The villagers of Treddoch are concerned with more important affairs, at least more important to them. In this village, the Solstice is just part of that longer and much more important period, 'The Season', as it's known.

The Season is that period of time which starts with Easter and lasts to the end of October. It's a period that has nothing to do with the Gregorian calendar as such but rather, their more particular almanac, the tourist one.

The Season's a shorter time frame than the calendar year altogether when those dependent on the tourist trade for their livelihood knuckle down to work. They have to make their living for the year as a whole in those few months. Once it's passed, if the opportunity's been missed, they know they won't have another chance till the following spring and there are always some that might not make it that far, economically speaking.


There are a fortunate few, of course, like Henry and Joan

from the Fudge Shop and Patience with her jewellery, who trade for different reasons. These are the ones who have alternative sources of income.

Patience trades for the company, the companionship that customers bring into her shop with them. That's why Patience is never in a hurry to close her shop of an evening. The money's an incidental. She hates the winter, when her shop's closed for weeks on end because of the lack of visitors and she's only The One-Eyed Dog for company.

Joan and Henry trade because, well, it just seemed a good idea at the time, certainly to Henry. It was all part and parcel of their moving to Cornwall, all part of their new life together. It's just as well that they've independent means though because it may have been a good idea to Henry, it certainly wasn't to Joan.

Joan hates serving the public; she's the sort of person who prefers to be served. Unlike Patience, Joan's always in a hurry to close the shop of an evening. One of Joan's ambitions is to sell the shop as soon as possible.

No, as far as the villagers are concerned the Solstice is just another sunrise on another day. There've been many before, both sunrises and solstices; there'll be more to come. The villagers, if nothing else, are pragmatic. To a man, using the term in a generic sense, they prefer their beds and their sleep for The Season's a period of long, hard work where days and weeks merge one into the other with little chance of respite.

The Captain, lying in his soft, down bed snores contentedly; his wife in unison. Yesterday was a long, hard day for them both and there's another one about to follow. The coming one will be particularly hard, for it's the one day of the week when The Captain accepts a coach party into his restaurant at lunchtime. In this case, it's yours, for the coming day is the highlight of your trip to Cornwall, a day in Treddoch Harbour.

You'll enjoy the experience, I'm sure though The Captain will be glad when it's over. Catering for over forty people, all at the same time is hard work. It's not that The Captain dislikes hard work, it's rather that he dislikes the meagre profit that he gets for this particular piece of work.

It's also a time of dreams, this Season, certainly a time when dreams stand the best chance of being fulfilled, for it's the time of year when the flow of money into the coffers is at full flood. Come the winter, the supply will be all but cut off as the source dries up; a veritable drought.

For the most part, these dreams that the villagers have are the sort of dreams that people everywhere have. They're as universal as the Solstice itself. There are dreams of husbands to be, of wives long lost, of loves, as yet unknown. For an older generation, there are dreams of grandchildren to come and, perhaps, a few more years to live. There are dreams of the material, of clothes and cars of boats and homes, of holidays to exotic places. There are also dreams of the more mundane.

Rachel, nestled nightly in Blossom Cottage, dreams of a foreign holiday and not just the Scillies either. When Rachael says, 'foreign' she means somewhere, with wall-to-wall sunshine and all-inclusive. She also has a fancy for a swimming pool that's warm to laze in, not like the local sea.

"It brings me out in goose pimples every time I go in;

even just thinking about it."

"But you never swim in the sea, not here."

"And now you know why!"

Her more practical husband points out that they need new windows this year. The ones they have, have finally rotted out.

"Can't you just patch them? You're good at that," she wheedles. Dreams of foreign shores are strong within her.

"What do you think I've been doing these last five years!" her husband replies, exasperated, and ponders the impractical nature of women.

As Blossom Cottage settles down Rachael dreams of lying on sun-blessed beaches, sitting in chairs under parasols, sipping something chilled from tall glasses and all, possibly, topless.

Her husband, on the other hand, dreams of oak sashes, so much sturdier than your basic pine he's inclined to think.

Adam, in the Old Post Office has thoughts of a new car, not a second-hand one this time, although he hasn't told his wife yet. She has dreams of her own. He's poured over brochures, checked out makes and models, considered colours. He just needs to earn the money for the deposit. The dream will drive him to succeed.

Andrew, a young man in his late twenties has visions of his own fishing boat. "I've had enough of crewing for somebody else," he tells the sea as he stands on the harbour wall, looking out towards the Eddystone. It's pretty much as far as Andrew ever travels, at least on land, apart from The Schooner Inn, that is.

He's already spoken to the Bank on the subject. The Manager has said to come back at the end of The Season, though he's not too worried. He knows it will be a sound investment. The boy's first love is the sea, his second will be his boat. As a bonus, from the Bank's perspective, Andrew still lives at home, with his parents, almost at the water's edge. His out-goings are minimal. There are certainly no travel-to-work costs to be considered.

There's also no woman in view either to put a strain on the boy's resources. That's at least, as far as The Manager knows, and he knows pretty much everything that goes on in the village. The Bank Manager's confident Andrew will be able to honour the repayments and if he does have problems, well, there's always mum and dad to call on.

Freya, in Holbourne House, dreams of new clothes, but then, Freya's thoughts are always on clothes despite any protestations to the contrary. Freya's dream is ongoing. She's a constant source of supply to the charity shop in the near-by town, though she declines to admit it.

"What! more clothes? You've only just bought some."

"That was ages ago. I've only got these few old rags. I haven't bought anything new for ages. I suppose you'd be happy to see me walking around in tatters." When he doesn't reply she quickly seizes the moment to add, "and shoes. Don't forget I'll need new shoes."

"Surely, you've got enough shoes. There are some in the back of your wardrobe that haven't seen the light of day in years," though why he bothers the arguing even he has to wonder. He knows, inherently, it's as futile as trying to stem the tide.

"No, I haven't and, anyway, a girl can never have enough shoes. Nor clothes."

"I'm sure they can," but this is said in a mumble.

If Freya's husband dreams of anything, it's most likely of a wife who's a bit less of a spendthrift; perhaps someone who might purchase from the charity shop on occasion as opposed to one inclined to help in keeping it fully stocked.

New anything. A treat. Something to be had at the end of The Season, paid for with their hard-won cash. The end of The Season, mind, not before. There's no certainty as to how the end might turn out until it arrives. They know that from experience.

For a few there are also dreams of the esoteric, of new adventures, of happier times, of more fulfilling lives.

Sitting in the Fishing Loft of an evening, nursing his pint, Darrel has dreams of travelling the world; of getting away for a while. He's unencumbered. "I want to see places I've only heard of. Places I've seen on the telly. Before it's too late." Given that Darrel's only just past eighteen it'll be a long time before it's too late for him but also, given his age, he sees twenty as being something of a watershed.

"Best go talk to The Captain then. He'll put you right. He'll know, The Captain," says one of Darrel's beer buddies, one no older than Darrel himself though someone knowledgeable on many matters, or so he likes to believe.

"Know what?"

"Places of course. Places to go. The Captain knows where everywhere is."

"How?"

"'Cos he's been everywhere."

"The Captain. Where?"

"Everywhere. You ask him. He used to skipper big ships. All around the world."

Two younger women who work the tables in one of the restaurants, discuss, as they pass, the joys of wedlock although, as yet, such joys are unknown to them and mostly gleaned from magazines.

"I want a husband. A ring on my finger. A home of my own."

"Me too. I'm fed up living with my parents."

Some women, on the other hand, ones that are now so encumbered, wish, perhaps, that they weren't. It's best, though, that their names are kept secret least their husbands should find out, for these are the women who wish their dreams hadn't visited them after all, all those years back, but had gone elsewhere.

"You can have my husband, with pleasure," says one.

"And mine. And my ring. I'll throw that in for nothing," adds a second. I want my old life back, the one I had before I was married, the one when I was free and single. No husband to run after day after day after day, like a servant. Cooking his meals, doing his washing. Staying in with the children whilst he goes out with his mates, down the Fishing Loft."

Dreams, like the weather, can change.


Lying locked in their separate sleeps as they are at this moment, in these early hours of a Midsummer's morning, in bedrooms throughout the village, which, with one or two expected exceptions, are their own, the inhabitants of Treddoch Harbour all dream their separate dreams, all hidden from curious view and all kept untold. These dreams are personal and for their dreamer's head only. Some of the dreams perhaps, are even more personal than others and certainly best kept hidden and secret. Rose's dream is such a one.

Rose is an eager young woman who just wants a short break in her life; from her life. She'd like an interlude, a short intermission; a little fling in fact. Nothing too serious of course; nothing that would lead to break-up and divorce. That would be a seismic shift. That's not what Rose wants at all. No, Rose just wants something, someone to brighten her day; make her feel special. Rose wants to be noticed again, as she'd once been noticed, before she was married.

Rose dreams of anything, anyone, although, in particular, Rose currently dreams of Rockabilly Joe. She visualises him stepping in to interrupt the monotony and boredom she feels that marriage has introduced, now that its first bright flushes have faded into what Rose perceives as dull, monotonous routine. Rose doesn't like dull and monotonous; dreaming provides her with an escape route. It's like tunnelling out of prison though, for Rose; half of the fun's in the tunnelling itself. She's not really thought it through as to what she might exactly do once she's the other side of the wire.

As for the older villagers, maybe they dream of years long past when life seemed simpler, more contented; dreams are very good at filtering out the unwanted. Perhaps they dream of having a few more years yet to come, for now, each, and every passing day becomes more precious to them as they close in on a conclusion.

Tom, in contrast to his contemporaries though, no longer dreams of years to come. He's had enough of the ones he's had. They've have been long and tedious to his way of thinking. Lonely too. He won't be sorry when they're over.

So, as they sleep, these villagers, on this most Midsummer of mornings they dream. Once their heads meet their pillows at night there's always a dream lying in wait ready to embrace and ensnare them. They have no choice but to receive it.

Treddoch Harbour's inhabitants though are slightly different from the mainstream of dreamers across the land, certainly in this one respect. Not only do they have their personal dreams, these villagers, they also have their communal dream.

This is the village dream, the corporate dream, the dream they all share, the one dream that binds them as a community, makes them a community. This is the dream of having 'A Good Season', for The Season's full upon them now and just about to move into a higher gear still, ready to hit overdrive.

How The Season unfolds will very much dictate to what degree their personal dreams will be fulfilled, at least for the many of them. To a greater or lesser extent, depending just how deeply they're entrenched in the tourist trade, their personal dreams are entwined with this corporate dream. For the many, they're inexorably linked, these two, the dreams and The Season.

So the days go on, both before and after Solstice; it's work and dream, work and dream. It's the dreams that sustain them, these villagers; it's the dreams that keep them burrowing. Such is the way of The Season.

This One Dream, the village dream, is the proverbial light, the exit strategy that keeps them burrowing day after interminable day, each day very much the same as the other. At this time there seems to be no beginning, no end. It's hard to differentiate between them, for there's little more to them other than toil and sleep, work and dream.

There is, however, also hope, hope that come the end, all their work won't have been in vain; money will have been made. If it has, then dreams can come true but for now, they're only halfway through, though the tourists are abroad, that much is certain. They're starting to swarm, much like the pilchards once did; all ready for the catch.

Just cast the net!

"Please, Lord, have mercy upon us. Let the sun shine, though not too much, otherwise, they'll all go to the beach instead of coming into our shops and cafés, our bars and restaurants, our ice cream stands. And if it must rain then, please Lord, let it be over-night for otherwise what will become of us when the long winter's months come, and we have nothing to show for it but empty purses."

As your coach heads for its destination, descending the steep hill that leads to the car park and village proper you'll notice that we can't help but pass by the cemetery to the left, standing, as it does, almost on the verge of the road on top of the hill here.

Normally, we wouldn't give the graveyard a second glance as we swish by in our air-conditioned comfort, would we? Nobody ever does, but, as we hurry past, bent and eager for more traditional sights let's spare a moment's thought for those buried in this well-walled patch of Cornish hillside. Though they now have been, these interred, they also still are whilst they remain in the memories of the living. Such memories are the boundary between the two realms, those of the living and the no longer.

For you, on this bus, the sun will shine, the rain will fall, the wind will blow but there, in that netherworld, in granite tombs and wooden boxes, neither night nor day is longer an option. Mornings never come; sunsets are notable only for their absence. Solstice has no meaning. Even food is a substance best forgotten for the smell of a pasty, piping from the oven, no longer stirs the senses there. Nothing does.

Whilst the memories hold though, the dead endure, if only for a while. They remain part of the fabric of the community still, and as such, all part of your coming day's experience. I can only recommend that we pause for just the shortest of whiles, so that you can meet a couple of the interred, by way of an introduction to Treddoch, before we scamper on and resume our itinerary. It will also help set the scene for you when you meet some of the other players later.

"One time, there were three butchers in the village; three mind you, just like there were three chapels," muses Butcher Trelawney, speaking through fixed lips, lying coffined as he is, side-by-side next to his once plump wife, she of the chubby arms, rosy cheeks and gold ringed fingers. It's the same wife who, now in death, is thin of body, due to a lack of flesh, and ringless, due to her daughter.

Unable to protest to the contrary, the Butcher's Wife had had her rings thoughtfully removed by her pinch-faced daughter, Tamsyn, before the girl consigned her mother to eternal twilight.

In fairness to Tamsyn, though she had shed a considerate tear, shown a suitably sad expression and all with a bowed head, in front of the congregation presently there assembled in the Chapel. It was only after that, and before the coffin lid was sealed that Tamsyn had, with the greatest of respect for her dead mother, removed the aforementioned rings for their safe-keeping.

"Well, they're no use to her where she's gone are they?" Tamsyn had said to her husband, Jack at the time, as much as anything a sop to her retreating conscience. "I might as well wear them, now. They are mine by rights after all, just like the butcher's shop, the house and the cottage down on the quay."

"I thought the butcher's shop was mine, now," said Jack, feeling suddenly side-lined. He was quickly getting used to the place being his domain, his own private area, even if it contained little more than a butcher's block, a sink and a cold store plus, of course, a selection of meat hooks. It was all very traditional.

"Indeed, you are the Butcher now, Jack," said Tamsyn, straitening Jack's tie and patting the pen in his top pocket. "And very smart you are too, blue striped and white-hatted. Every chop and shin a butcher through and through. But *I* own the shop; the deeds are in my name. The shop's *mine* now; *I* inherited it," and she mentally ticks it off of her asset list.

There's also their house, formerly belonging to her grandparents, then her parents, the cottage down on the quay, formerly belonging to her parents, then her and the gold rings, formerly belonging to her mother, now hers also. Tamsyn's also recently started to add Jack to her list. For the moment, Jack's considered to be an asset.

There would have been the old slaughterhouse too, if her father hadn't sold it to 'them foreigners', as Tamsyn tends to refer to the Developer From London and his wife. She never refers to them by name. Goodness only knows what her Granfer might have said, she often wonders. Tamsyn would tut and shake her head in memory of what she felt her grandfather would have thought.

Tamsyn, it should be noted, doesn't resemble her late mother in looks one bit, thin where her mother was more rotund. In fact, Tamsyn rather favours her late grandfather in that respect, a man she still idolises. As well as being similar in build they both also had a great respect for money; especially for keeping hold of it.

"And the bundles of notes in the old tin under the bed," added Jack, somewhat wistfully and with just an edge of bitterness. He'd barely glanced them before Tamsyn had skitted them away to a new hidey-hole of which only she knew and kept the key around her neck to prove it.

"Be quiet, you fool. Do you want everyone to know?" though there was no one else in the shop at that moment, other than the three of them, Jack, Tamsyn and a certain air of disquiet.

"I thought they did," he muttered as well as some other, unheard comments, under his breath; comments, which if they had have been heard could have reduced his privileges for a week. At the very least. To relieve his frustrations, Jack cleaved a piece of beef bone with the force of a southwest gale heaving the Atlantic at the palisade of rock that serves to protect the little village from its plundering path.

The beef bone wasn't so fortunate.

"And a slaughterhouse too," the old Butcher contemplates, in his endless cascade of death-induced murmurings. He thinks of the slaughterhouse in its heyday, when cows and pigs and sheep all went in and their clean skinned carcasses came out, becoming chops and roasts for his customers.

All this was in a time before Jason, the Pie and Pasty Maker had moved into the premises next door but one. Jason had never known the slaughterhouse in its heyday though he'd always bought his meat from The Butcher none-the-less. You could always count on the quality of Butcher Trelawney's meats even if, in those later days, The Butcher hadn't personally selected the animal prior to slaughter.

In return, The Butcher had always had a fresh-baked pie with his crib every morning, ten o'clock, regular as his bowel movements. A cup of tea and a meat pie from Jason.

Ten o'clock could be a busy time of day in the Butcher's. Some days his cup of tea would be as cold as his fridge, but he didn't mind. It just meant he'd been busy, so there'd be money in the till by way of compensation.

Butcher Trelawney liked the Pie Maker's pies and, anyway, it made good business sense, didn't it for, after all, the Pie Maker did buy the meat from him. So The Butcher returned the favour. In addition, knowing where the content had come from, the Butcher knew too that the filling was fresh to boot. There was nothing unsavoury in The Butcher's savoury as it were.

As he lies in his grave, stone-stiff, The Butcher remembers his till too. It was once music to his now muted ears. Mentally, he remembers hearing the coins peel like Christian bells, cascading as they did from his hands into their many compartments. Sadly, to The Butcher's way of thinking, they were taken out again all too soon by his cheerlessly chubby wife for their shopping. It was to pay for the milk, the newspapers, the coal and such like, she'd said. She forgot to mention, of course, it was also to pay for her once growing collection of gold rings.

"But it was my only pleasure and vice, as you well know," says The Butcher's Wife. "Not like some, as I could mention. Behind the clubhouse, up on the cliffs, even in the old net house, so I've heard tell. And you have too if you'd but admit it."

The Butcher had and did and thought a thought, and a sinful thought it was too in his otherwise God-fearing, if now empty, head.

"Every Saturday night, come rain or shine there they'd be, drunk out of mind, not that they ever had any. Wobbling away, they were, in their heels; all faux fur and no knickers. I sat home with you, remember teetotaller and God-fearing man that you were. Not that it did you much good in the end though, did it? All those Sundays, handing out hymn books at the Chapel door, wearing your trouser knees as thin as your hair with your praying, singing like a linnet, albeit a slightly tuneless one, and did He repay you for your devoutness? No! Not one bit. Not a jot. Treated just like the rest we've been. Worse than the rest in fact. They're still alive. Look at us. Just look at us, Butcher."

There's little need 'to look' for The Butcher's all too aware of their circumstances having lain next to these incessant jabberings for however long now and with no means of ever escaping. Locked together with Mrs Trelawney for all eternity, perhaps even beyond, isn't a comforting thought to The Bucher.

In life, the Butcher's Wife had held a view on the afterlife that was both as naive in its thinking as it was in its explanation. She'd been a great believer in there being an eternal book of souls, although exactly where this book was held, she never did venture an opinion. Everyone's deeds were recorded in it. Come the end, when the results were totted up it would be decided whether blessings or punishments were to be meted out.

The Butcher's Wife had always thought that she and The Butcher leaned more to the positive side of the ledger, what with them being Chapel goers, tea-total and all that. Letting the rest of the village know her views on the subject only sweetened her perceptions the more. It was one reason, of course, for many of the locals to shop early, before The Butcher's Wife appeared in the shop and soured their day or later on before The Butcher had completed his final clean, but after Mrs. Trelawney had returned home.

"There I was, looking forward to a long and happy life, and suddenly…" She trails off and would give her head a sad shake if she was still able. "Look at us now Butcher, interred together. Here!"

The Butcher noiselessly groans at such a dark, dire thought. He clearly must have been more sinful than he could possibly have ever imagined. If that was the case then there was, clearly, no way of making amends now. Justice's scales seem to have been weighed more heavily against him than he'd ever realised.

"'Taken Before Their Time', it says on the slab above our heads."

"That's what it says, Butcher, and so we were. One minute I remember ogling, rather, admiring, a somewhat splendid diamond ring in The Jewellers, there in the city. It was that autumn Saturday afternoon, remember. You thought you'd caught a chill. You couldn't stop sneezing. What a fuss you made about it when it was no more than a sniffle."

"I remember us on our way to the Greek restaurant for a bite to eat too. After that, it's all a bit blank for the very next thing I find is us, here, side by side without even a ring to polish. My rings, taken before their time too!"

Butcher Trelawney vaguely recalls; being dead his memory's no longer what it was. It was late autumn and he had caught a chill; he didn't 'think' he had, and it wasn't 'a sniffle' either. It was a full-on cold, not that his wife was in any way sympathetic. She'd had her own agenda that day.

The Butcher had felt shivery-cold all morning as he worked his shop and had been glad it was Saturday; early closing. He'd been looking forward to staying at home, lighting a fire and settling in before its warmth, his feet up, toasting them, like he did his bread.

But no, it wasn't to be; his wife had gone on and on as to how she never went anywhere, never did anything. Stuck in the village, day after day, she'd said. Was it too much to ask, she'd continued, that he take her to the city? It was only for the afternoon. He could sit in front of his fire as much as he liked when they returned. It was only the once-in-a-while after all, she'd wheedled. The old Butcher had found it easier to acquiesce than argue, particularly given how his head was feeling. Perhaps he should have argued his case a bit more, he's now inclined to think.

On the drive home the road was wet from intermittent, but heavy, showers. There was a low sun, directly in his face, as he crested the hill on the main road, it's light reflecting from the tarmacked surface as it would from any mirror. It had blurred his vision which was blurred enough already from the head-cold his wife had refused to acknowledge. She was wittering on about another ring; diamond this time wasn't it? Yes, he remembers that. He also remembers having a sneezing fit. He had been right, he had caught a chill.

Clearly distracted, one way and another, he'd failed to hear the screams of his spouse, the raucous sound of blaring horns or notice the forty-ton of motorised steel that he'd all too leisurely veered into the path of until it was, as is now proven, too late.

It was fortunate, for Tamsyn that is, though not her parents, that the accident had happened not too late on that fateful Saturday afternoon for the emergency services had excelled themselves in notifying her with an unexpected degree of promptness. This was mainly due to the fact that a member of the constabulary, and on duty at the time, was a local boy himself. To him fell the task of breaking the news, though he noted that Tamsyn had borne it all with a fortitude greater than might generally have been expected, as he mentioned to his mother, later that evening, when off duty.

In Chapel, next morning, The Constable's Mother couldn't help but keep glancing Tamsyn's way, her son's words echoing in her head. She'd never really taken to the child, even as a baby. She'd always felt there was an unpleasant side to the girl. Took after her grandfather, The Old Butcher, in that too, The Constable's Mother had thought. It cheered the woman to have her earlier suppositions proven correct when she looked across at the girl; proven at least to her satisfaction.

From the organisational perspective, the timing of the accident had meant that Tamsyn could start to get affairs somewhat in order on the Sunday, straight after Chapel. The funeral director, though business based in the nearby town, is a member of the congregation here, an old friend of her late parents, and the Minister, of course, being Sunday, was obviously to hand and able to extend immediate condolences.

He would visit again later in the week, he'd confirmed, and had duly turned-up as promised, with prayer book, as always, in hand. Whether he carries the book to provide succour to himself or his flock is never certain.

Jack, unexpectedly promoted from Assistant to Butcher,

literally over-night, somewhat to his surprise, could, according to Tamsyn, open the shop as normal on the Monday morning. There was no point in missing trade was there. After all, it wasn't going to help her parents, having the shop closed, was it?

Opening the shop Tamsyn was sure was what her father would have wanted; Granfer surely would have. Being practical it would also kill the proverbial birds for Jack could accept the condolences of the locals, along with their monies for their post-weekend purchases, both at the same time.

That the funeral was going to be an expensive affair was Tamsyn's first thought, though one she could hardly escape, wish as she might. After all, her parents had had a position not only in the local community, they'd been stalwarts of the Chapel to boot. It was an expense that had to be borne with resilience and fortitude.

However, the sudden realisation that she could soon recoup the outgoings several times over caused an almost smile to breach Tamsyn's face as her mind grasped the opportunity to turn a profit.

Quite simply, she and Jack would move into her, now late, parents' home (suddenly vacant) and she'd rent out their cottage on the quay come the next Season. A brilliant plan, even if she said so herself and one which helped calm her mind over the expenses about to be incurred.

Jack's opinion was neither sought nor required. He was moved to the new residence along with the rest of the belongings, which, as was clearly noted, were all Tamsyn's, apart from the odd, few personal effects that Jack might have had. They didn't amount to much.

"I sat with you and polished my rings till they gleamed with a shine that would have made an angel's halo look tarnished. It was my only sin, Butcher. Surely I should have been allowed one sin."

The Butcher can't disagree with that. They all had at least one sin after all. Some, indeed, had a few more than that. Clearly, given his present predicament, he must have been one in the latter category though, for the life of him, or, should that be the death of him, he ponders, he can't think what. As far as he can recall he'd always led a pretty, blameless life; at least to his way of thinking.

"Rough and ready they were too," adds The Butcher's Wife through her cold, boned lips. "and some more ready than others! Especially that Trevail girl, all blonde dyed and short-skirted. She could never say no, even if she wanted to, brazen hussy as she is." The Butcher's Wife mentally shrugs her death stiff shoulders at her thoughts.

"Not that I think she ever wanted to say no. Always laughing and smiling. Constantly cheerful. It's not natural that's for sure. Nobody can be that happy! Look at our Tamsyn."

The Butcher would rather not for, as the years had passed, Tamsyn seemed to be happiest only when miserable. He could see, Tamsyn was following his father somewhat in that regard as well as with her attachment to her pennies.

As a child, Tamsyn's piggy bank had only ever been seen when coins were entering at the top. For them to be removed via the rubber plug at the bottom was an infrequent event and rarely ever witnessed, undertaken in secret as it generally was.

Butcher Trelawney's father, Old Butcher Trelawney, was well noted in his time for his carefulness, or meanness as some preferred to call it. It was rumoured that he was so tight with his money that he'd wash his condoms out for further use, hanging them in the airing cupboard to dry. Although this was generally considered to be only a rumour there were a couple of older villagers who swore they knew the truth of it.

It was also rumoured that, when he had died, his son had found an old tea chest in the attic, stuffed with cash. It was never confirmed, of course. Nobody wanted the taxman snooping around. The Excise had never been made welcome in Cornwall and Young Butcher Trelawney had seen no need to go against tradition.

What was certainly true though, and well known throughout Treddoch, was the fact that after his wife had died the Old Butcher would sit in his overcoat of a winter's evening rather than light a fire, his sitting room lit only by the dismal glow of a forty-watt light bulb hanging from the centre of the ceiling. The Old Butcher had never seen a need to squander money unnecessarily.

Lying in his coffin Butcher Trelawney thinks of 'that Trevail girl', as his wife now disparagingly refers to Elizabeth, as she was called at birth, though Lizzy ever thereafter. The Butcher's opinion of her has always differed to his wife's; he'd always thought Lizzy to be a lovely, lovely girl. He remembers her electric smile that lifted his mornings, every time she swirled into his shop.

"Morning Mr. Trelawney. I think I'll have a pork chop today please." Always so polite and well-mannered to boot. "And some sausages for the Little People. I'm sure they'd live on sausage and beans if I'd let them." And a laugh would peel from her.

He'd known Lizzy since she was born; her parents too. Although not Chapel people they were nice enough for all that The Butcher had always thought; kind and helpful too. They'd always do anybody a good turn if asked; even without being asked, which was more than could be said for many, Butcher Trelawney had to confess. They'd hearts of a diamond clarity he'd always felt, especially Lizzy's mother. Her father's a quiet chap who's worked hard all his life. The Butcher had had a great respect for him, for the both of them in fact.

They'd both known Lizzy, The Butcher and his Wife since she was born. She was the same age as Tamsyn. The two girls had started school together and had been close friends once. They could always be seen deep in whispers as they'd walked arm-in-arm along the road to school in the morning and back again at teatime and were always around each other's homes, after school, at weekends, or in the holidays.

Time is transient though; there's nothing known that's forever. The world spins on its axis, it never forgets, and as it spins people grow, transform, transmogrify even. They change from what they were to what they come to be.

So it was too, with the girls that had been so close; as women, they became so distant. They've become so distant in fact that, if they're to move any further apart, they're likely to come back towards each other from the opposite direction. That's how far apart they now are.

They'd grown apart slowly, almost imperceptibly at first as they'd moved through early teens, but the process had speeded up as their teens ended. Lizzy began to embrace life with the love and passion normally reserved for those with an evangelical zeal whilst Tamsyn, raven of hair, beaked of nose, and with a sharp chin grew into a thinner, meaner version of her grandfather and even more purposeful in her pursuit of the pennies. Tight of everything in general, Tamsyn was particularly tight of purse.

Although still only in her latter twenties there are the first signs of grey in Tamsyn's hair which she refuses to address, accepting what is as is. Jack would prefer it if she did something about it and thinks of Lizzy's contrasting blonde locks, somewhat too wistfully.

Happiness to Tamsyn has always been a healthy bank account and a strong asset book of which a husband is considered to form a part of. Love and looks are severely overrated in Tamsyn's opinion, generally considered an irrelevance and, as such, are recorded on the debit side.

Tamsyn had married Jack more as part of a business plan really, rather than a romance whilst Lizzy has continued, blissfully single. She's been content, at least until now, with her two Little People and lack of a permanent male presence. As has already been noted though, everything's up for change.

As she lies, earth cold, beneath the Cornish dirt and wet, with only worms and a dead husband for company, The Butcher's wife dreams of Saturday night sins that might have been. Nights where she could have incurred feats behind the paint-peeled clubhouse, up on moon drenched cliffs or in the dusty, dank old net house, wearing little more than a short, tight skirt, fishnets and stiletto heels.

Danny would have been up for it she knows. He'd always had a fancy for her, ever since school days. The Butcher's wife had had a crush on him too. Sadly, for Danny though, he didn't have a Butcher's business to inherit, let alone a cottage on the quay ready to move into just as soon as Butcher Trelawney (Young Butcher Trelawney that is) was to marry.

Old Butcher Trelawney had been shrewd, setting up the path for his son to walk soon after the boy's birth. The Butcher's Wife had liked that; she'd always admired the old man's business acumen; his firm grasp on the pennies which had so readily led to the pounds. So, she did the only sensible thing, she tells herself, with a soundless sigh and had married The Young Butcher.

She was content too, she consoles herself. What's good with just being happy. Happiness doesn't pay the bills, nor put rings on your fingers was her thought on the matter. "Though that Trevail girl does seem to get by," and she thinks, a thought tinged with a bitterness, both for Lizzy's ability 'to get by' and her own present predicament.

For his part, Butcher Trelawney thinks nostalgically of the old slaughterhouse he'd sold for a song, and a sad song it was at that, to a blue-eyed, fast-talking, money throwing Developer From London with a silver sports car of certain distinction and an overly prettied wife in chic clothing.

The car was a somewhat older model, though in truth, much could have been said of the wife. Both she and the sports car had seen better days, but they still held enough appeal to charm the villagers, certainly Butcher Trelawney, and that was all the Developer From London was interested in. For all their talk of 'moving down', 'settling in', 'wanting to be part of the community' it was just as much hot air as came from the exhaust of the aging sports and as noxious too.

"It's just a row of cottages now; and a short row at that. Just the three, in fact. Hardly a row at all. Not very pretty ones either," he muses.

Thank God his father had died before he'd done the deal; the Lord alone knows what Old Butcher Trelawney would have said at his son's ineptitude. But then, Butcher Trelawney never was the businessman his father had been as some in the village had been wont to point out; his wife included.

To make matters worse, at least to the Butcher's mind, once the offending properties had been built, they were sold, for exorbitant sums, to foreigners from as far afield as Swindon and St Albans, one even from Stoke. The Developer From London then upped sticks and moved with sports car and wife to whatever project next held his attention.

They never did settle in the village at all. They'd never had any intention, as The Butcher finally came to realise.

"Where's my old slaughterhouse now?" asks The Butcher, of himself.

"And my rings?" asks The Butcher's Wife.

A tear would run down The Butcher's eyeless socket, if it only could, in sorrow for days now gone. There's now no till to ring, no Lizzy to brighten his mornings and no slaughterhouse to gaze on with the satisfaction that the property is still his.

Death's a bitch, he might think, were it not for his Chapel upbringing, where such thinking was not to be encouraged.

# Very Early Morning

It's questionable whether this point of our visit, where the dark and light are about to merge, can be deemed as being termed as early morning or end of the night. The best that can be said of it is that it's somewhere on the cusp. One thing that is certain though, whatever the opinion on the semantics, it's still far too early for the shore-sided stay-a-beds of Treddoch Harbour.

They'll do their best to ignore the early, Midsummer light and hug their pillows to the very last, fearing the alarm as much this morning as any other morning. At this point, they're as innocent as new-borns, being in the full depth of sleep as they are, lightly buried under summer duvets, hidden away, safe, for the moment, from the impending day and all that it therein entails.

One such stay-a-bed is Molly Pendarritt, spinster of the parish. Like the rest of the villagers she too is tucked into a dream, though, unlike them, hers is not connected to The Season for Molly's Head Teacher in the local primary school.

Molly has everything she personally wants from life except for one thing which is why, each and every night as she tucks-up, Molly dreams of having a husband. Hers is a dream that recurs with an unfailing exactitude, whatever the time of year for, as yet, it's still an unrequited dream.

Molly, now in her later thirties continues to live alone, unless you count her cat, Bastet, as companion. Even that's questionable, for Bastet is her own person, using that term in its widest and loosest sense. Bastet tends to come and go as she pleases, treating Molly's cottage as little more than a hotel, full board and lodging included. Bastet even has her own set of keys, so to speak.

Bastet's an unusual name for a cat you might think and would be right, but we can come to that later.

Bastet is an independent soul, an old soul in fact, or so Molly claims. It's certainly true that the village seems to be her domain, one in which she wanders at will for no other cats bother her; even the dogs give her a wide berth.

Bastet appeared early, one sun-slippered morning, though no one knew from where; no one had seen sight of her previously. She'd just appeared, as if the result of a magic trick it might have seemed; pulled from a top hat.

She'd sat and waited patiently outside of the lightly rusting gate that marks the boundary between the pathway and Molly's cottage of slate and stone, a short, cobbled path connecting the two.

There's a stable door too, under the porch, designed specifically so that Molly can leave the top half part open to welcome in the summer light and heat whilst retaining some semblance of privacy. It hides her away, at least to a degree, from inquisitive eyes of passing visitors keen to catch a glimpse of a cottage interior to add to their experiences.

The Cat, as Bastet has also become known, had sat and waited patiently, with a mournful expression welded to her face, until Molly had opened her morning door to let in the day.

"Well, hello," said Molly softly from over the top of the

stable door. "And who are you? Who do you belong to? I haven't seen you around here before. Are you hungry?"

Questions, questions, questions. "Of course, I'm hungry," thought The Cat eager to progress things whilst doing her best to maintain the tragic look. She didn't want to rush the gate, let alone jump over the low wall that ran beside it, although that was something she could have easily accomplished with little more than the twitch of a whisker. No, she'd wait, she didn't want to seem too eager, not just yet. She had the human hooked; she sensed that. It was all about reeling her in now.

Molly edged slowly forward, murmuring buttermilk-soft words as she went; all creamy and encouraging. She didn't want to frighten the little feline, not realising that she couldn't. The Cat, forged from carbon steel, had already decided that this was to be her new home.

Molly opened the creaky gate slowly, and with just a more than normal extra touch of care. The Cat, stock still, sat for just that moment, cautioning herself against an over-eagerness.

"Come on then," said Molly, indicating the open door, sheltered beneath its porch. It was framed on either side with patches of cornflowers of the palest blues and pinks, interspersed with white and backed by hollyhocks, the colours of a fine Burgundy. It was picture perfect, a gift-in-waiting to the snap-happy tourists that would be arriving later. For The Cat, uninterested in any of that, it was simply, game, set and match.

Bastet, as she was to be known, straightened her shoulders and erected her tail to regal height, giving it just the slightest curl at the top, purely for style. She fixed her stare on the opening ahead and let the mask of vulnerability slide from her face. With the stately grace of one used to attendants-in-waiting, Bastet sauntered down the short, paved path and into the cottage, leaving Molly, servant-like, to close both gate and door behind them.

Molly's an educated woman, very educated, which, some in the village say, is the reason why she still lives alone.

Molly's also an avid reader, another reason, others suggest, as to why she still lives alone.

She's not one to frequent the local pubs on a regular basis, either, as many of her old friends still do. That's not to say that Molly objects to the odd glass or two, but she does prefer wine, generally a chilled white. It's further evidence, so yet others believe, as to why Molly retains her singularity in life.

So the cat was named, from the well-depths of Molly's knowledge, her knowledge of old folklore in general and of Egyptology in particular and, as it happened, the naming has suited well.

It hadn't taken long for Bastet to establish expected parameters, in particular, what she would tolerate and what she wouldn't. The latter included a yappy-type dog some visitor had brought to the holiday cottage next door and which now bears a permanent scar on the end of its inquisitive nose. If nothing else it should prove a useful reminder to it, for future reference, to respect another's personal space.

There are also items in the cottage that are now recognised as specific to Bastet such as her chair. There's also Bastet's spot on the hearth where she likes to recline in front of a winter's fire and her space on the lounge window sill, from which ornaments have had to be removed in order to make room for her to take a view of the outside world.

There's also a particular position in the kitchen, where she prefers to have her food bowl placed.

Bastet now even has her own entrance, technically speaking. Molly refers to it as a 'cat flap', a term Bastet regards with some disdain whenever she hears it mentioned. To Bastet, it's a doorway to freedom, access to the outer world as and when *she* chooses and Bastet does like to come and go as she pleases. The Cat sees herself bound to no one, independent as she is, a free spirit.

Unbound, independent, free? Well, to a point. Bastet is prepared to make an exception come mealtimes, of course. At such times Bastet will sell her feline soul for a little plastic pouch of pure pleasure bought by Molly from the local store each day.

Better still, of course, are the days when she's given a nice piece of salt-fresh fish taken straight from the sea that very morning. The local fishermen tend to spoil her as does Molly who steams it to a perfection seldom seen in the best restaurants. Bastet has now become very particular and very demanding.

"For goodness sake do have some patience," scolds Molly as the cat, excited by the fiendishly, fishy smells, emanating from somewhere way above her silky head, weaves and twines her way through Molly's legs threatening disaster should Molly let her mind wander for even an instance.

But scold as she might, Molly's glad of even Bastet's wanton company. It's better than being completely alone.


Despite the various theories proffered, it's difficult to pinpoint exactly why Molly is so alone. She's not unattractive after all, in fact, quite the opposite. She's also a mild temperament and easy disposition.

It's hard to understand why she has no man to snuggle against at night and no man to cook and clean for. She'd willingly do that, she says. Why is it that there's no man to sit with by a winter's fire, listening together to the sou'-west winds, rampaging their paths through the village as they twist between houses, race down chimneys, and continue their unending search for cracks between glass and frame? Why is there no one to sit close with as the rain beats with ferocious fists against the thin glazed window panes of her ancient cottage?

Molly can never understand why she has no man to walk with across a summer's cliff. She can never understand why there's no man to buy her an indulgent ice cream or share an evening bag of chip-shop chips as they would sit tight together on the harbour wall, under a setting sun. She'd dearly love to be with someone, laughing, chortling as they fended off the seagulls that, stealth-like, would creep their way forward, heads cocked to one side, but with covetous eyes on the chips, always on the chips. A careless move and one would be gone. The whole bag if the gulls were lucky!

Worst of all Molly finds it difficult to understand why she has no one to sit with and listen to the breathing of babies that seem increasingly unlikely to be.

No, a cat for companion would seem to be the best that Molly can hope for, but, like the other villagers, come bedtime, Molly too can dream.

Part way along the path that cuts across the cliffs on the eastern side of the village, just past the last of the houses that line the

route, there's a urine scented shelter. It overlooks the harbour where the boats, at this early hour, lie beached and quiet, unwanted and unattended, till the morning tide. It's still very early morning remember; the clock hasn't ticked all that far into the new day just yet.

Johnny, to his drinking companions, 'that useless, useless bastard,' to his once loving wife, lies in the shelter, sprawled on the wood hard bench, comatose, unfeeling of the aches the planks are inflicting on his body, numbed as it still is from last night's anaesthetics; too many of them. Last night there were far, far too many, even by Johnny's standards and Johnny can quaff when necessary. He's fully qualified to a master's level.

"I should have listened to my mother," says Abi, his long-suffering wife, time after endless time. "She was right; she knew what you were like. She said you were idle; you'd always be idle. She said you'd never change."

"Your father was idle," adding, as an afterthought, "God rest his soul," in deference to his now non-earthly status. "You're just like him and your brother's not much better, though he does keep a job. That's something I suppose. More than you do anyway. If it wasn't for your poor mother, slaving herself to the bone, goodness knows what would have become of you all. A hopeless bunch, the three of you!"

When Abi's in one of her rants Johnny has the good sense to keep his mouth closed and accept the lashes with fortitude. Even he can recognise them as his due punishment.

"Well I don't intend ending up like her, so don't think I do. What's she to show for it all? A drunk of a husband, dead drunk as he now is, and a drunk of a son. I thank the Lord every day that we've not been blessed. I should have hated any child of mine turning out like you."

So her outbursts would go, time following endless time though, so far, to little effect. Johnny is still Johnny and unchanged though change, as yet unrealised, is in the offing.

In these early hours we find Johnny's life to be on the point of transformation, although, it's fairly certain, that he's not actually fully aware of it as yet. Given his current state, Johnny's not actually aware of anything though.

There are forces and influences, well outside of his control, that are about to act upon him. One such is Abi. There is, after all, only so much a girl can take, and Abi has taken much. She's all but reached her limit.

Abi, the once pretty Abi, was a girl known for her soft, sweet smile and blue-green eyes which, under Jonny's artistic bent, had flashed and sparkled as luminescent as the glow from a burning sun reflected on a Treddoch sea in his paintings of her.

Sadly, after several years with Johnny Abi's now a girl with signs of tear and wear around the edges of both smile and eyes. There've been too many years of trying to make a home for them both, working as a barmaid at night, part-time in the local shop of a day, cleaning cottages of a Saturday morning. For all her anguishing and avowals though, Abi isn't really that pleased that she hasn't had a child, even if it had turned out to be like Johnny.

"Better that even than be childless," she would whisper to herself, crying bitter, as she constantly did, for her emptiness. "What's going to become of me? Who's to comfort me? Be a companion. Not that useless bastard, that's for sure. He can't even look after himself.

"Having Johnny's like having a child, only worse. At least

with a child, there's hope for their future. What hope is there with him?" and she would look down at her hands as she wrung them in her lap.

Abi would like to have had a baby despite her protestations to the contrary; that's her wish. A cuddlesome, troublesome baby to coddle and fuss over, to walk to school every morning and then to walk back with every afternoon. Rain or shine it wouldn't matter. She'd see they were properly dressed; sandals for sun, wellies for rain and pretty shoes for the in-between bits, if it was a girl. She hadn't quite given thought to what a boy might wear on such occasions.

It would be nice to have a little one to go to sports days and carol services with, to harvest festivals and summer fairs, just like some of her friends did. It would be fun to make hats for the Maypole dancing, help with homework and organise end-of-term cards for teachers. There were so many things that could have been but weren't and as things stood, most likely, never would be.

Johnny Polmayne (John as he was actually Christened, John Hedley Polmayne, the 'Hedley' after his maternal grandfather) is, by all accounts, including his own on the few occasions he's honest with himself, a no-good wastrel. He's little more than a poser, a weaver of dreams that, at the moment of meeting, he's unlikely ever bring to substance, due mostly to a degree of idleness which he has personally taken to the level of an art form alongside that of his painting.

Johnny accepts his faults as truth, at least in his more lucid moments, which are, at best, fleeting. His is a tortured soul, or so Johnny tells himself for he's a painter, an artist of prodigious potential but one, according to his own vindication, still looking for his muse.

Johnny can always find an excuse for his present position rather than just getting on with life like most people which is all rather sad for, when he does set his mind to it, Johnny's an artist of outstanding talent. That, perhaps, is the source of his problems, apart from his drinking, of course.

Johnny had thought he'd found his muse in Abi, those so many years ago and, truth to tell, it might have been, had he been bold enough to grasp and grapple it, give it the energy it demanded from him but Johnny's weak of will. He lacks spirit and's prone to taking the stress-free route, running from anything that demands his undivided attention; running even from himself. In a word, Johnny's idle.

Johnny's mother was right, even he's had to confess. He does take after his father. Idle through to the heart, the pair of them and drinkers to boot. They've both preferred the easy way out of life; it was quite literal in his father's case.

Johnny's father! He was a man who could drink with the best of them, though a man who'd never made old bones; the alcohol had seen to that.

Bleared of vision and wavering on his feet, he'd stepped backward, one moonless night, from the quay's edge just a tad too far. He'd dropped stone-like, hitting the rocky, waterless bottom of the harbour with the dullest of thuds, catching his head, just for good measure, on the white wooded bow of an all too solid boat as he'd plummeted southwards. He was, officially, dead drunk.

Now he lies atop of the village, killed by the drink that he'd so dearly loved. He's near to Butcher Trelawney though, in contrast, left scant all behind to show for his brief tenure of the Earth but a once beered breath, rounded belly, and empty pockets.

Johnny's Father, who had never said much of sense or note when he was alive, says nothing now for he lies cold and alone. There's no one sufficiently interested in his remains to put even the fewest of flowers on his desolate grave, most certainly not his widow who's probably grateful for the peace he's given to the both of them. Even the white stonecrop, generally so prolific throughout the cemetery, avoids it, as one might a leper.

Johnny doesn't want to end up like his father he sometimes thinks, though most often not, think that is. This is especially true when he's in the bar of The Schooner Inn, ambitiously named, as it was, in time past.

As far as is known no schooner had or has ever actually visited the village. Rather, they'd sailed majestically past, their prows in the air, snubbing such a small inlet as they headed for the safety of the city's breakwater. They'd also preferred the city for its brighter lights, larger life, and looser women as against anything that the chapel-encrusted harbour of Treddoch could offer.

Once inside, supping an ale or three, Johnny's soon cocooned from life in an intoxicated blissfulness being feted by equally befuddled friends and visitors alike. They're happy to ply him with a pint as the price of a good yarn, and Johnny has a few of those to tell, though, by now, they've become so far stretched from the original as to have become fairy tales in their own right.

As well as an artist, Johnny's also a master magician, a caster of spells, which he casts over everyone, likeable as he is. How else did Abi fall for him, she sometimes wonders?

Knowing the reception most definitely awaiting his return to the domestic hearth Johnny had decided, following closing time, and with a speed that belied the addled numbness of his brain, to sleep for just an hour or so in the shelter. This would provide time, so Johnny calculated, for Abi to be tucked safely in bed and, hopefully, fast asleep. He could recite the expected conversation he would otherwise encounter; as predictable as the coming and going of the tides.

One thing Johnny hadn't predicted though, was just how deep a sleep all that ale was to plunge him into; certainly more than an hour or two. Johnny never can get things right.

"Just like your father. Why your mother married him, goodness only knows. But then, why did I marry you?"

"Smooth talkers, both of you. Charming. Good looking. Ok, ok!" and here she would dramatically hold her hands up, palms forward. "Ok, ok, so I made the same mistake as your mother, didn't I? But it can't go on forever, Johnny, it can't! I'm not your mother. It's bad enough just being your wife and it's getting to the point that I don't think I want to be for much longer, I really don't."

Abi would break into sobs at this point which would, in turn, break his heart for Johnny knows, at these times, that Abi speaks the truth. If nothing else he does love Abi and despises himself for what he puts her through. Worst of all he despises himself for not being able, or even prepared to make any attempt, to change.

Johnny knows that, someday, it will all come to an end if he carries on the way he is at the moment and the end is coming well into view. Even he can see the beginnings of it. Abi, he knows, isn't bluffing. She's perfectly right, she isn't his mother; She's made of sterner stuff. Abi's still young, though at times like these she doesn't feel it. She wants a life, not an existence. She won't accept his nonsense for much longer and the nonsense has already been going on for far too long as it is.

Unfortunately, Johnny struggles to cope with the realities of life, especially when as soused as a herring. So, with discretion being the better part of valour (though Johnny was too far gone for that depth of thinking last night) he'd felt that it would be better to face the wrath that was sure to come later, much, much later. So much later in fact that perhaps, just perhaps, Abi's caustic tone might have tempered, even a little. He would have happily settled for just 'abrasive'. As well as being useless, Johnny's also a coward at heart.

To Abi, the years past are now a world away. Then, they were ones of feelings, of futures, of hopes and of promises. There'd been thoughts of a pretty, chocolate box cottage of their own, a baby polished to perfection in a buggy outside a sun-soaked door, a cat, sitting porcelain-like in the windowsill, staring at tides and tourists alike. That had been Abi's dream. Back then she'd even thought of a name for him, the cat that had never happened, much like the baby and the cottage and everything else.

All Abi has to show for these ten lost years is a bare bank account, a hollowed heart and, tucked away in the back of a cupboard some portraits that Johnny had painted of her in that brief, brief moment when she'd believed that she was his muse. In return, Abi had believed all of Johnny's promises; love had smeared a lustre over everything.

Like the rest of the villagers, Johnny too has a dream, in his case one of being a talented, successful artist and, in his case, it's a dream that could be. It has plausibility if only Johnny would set himself to the task.

Tonight though, or rather, this morning, lying supine as he is, where he is, Johnny's dream is far removed from its norm. It's being usurped by one of pain and torture, an unusual and unnatural dream for Johnny. Johnny's dreams are usually more pastoral; they're never this aggressive.

This time, Johnny's dreaming has taken a sideways shift. He's being, tortured though not of his artistic soul but his body. He can feel the pain, pure and physical as if it's for real.

The pain he dreams he's feeling is coming from sharp needles, being pushed rhythmically into his chest whilst the odour of oily fish that's assaulting his nostrils is making his now delicate stomach nauseous in the extreme. He could retch from the smell. To compound it all there's a steady, pulsing sort of hum in the background. The only problem is, this isn't a dream; the torture Johnny's experiencing as he lies prone is for real.

As Johnny's brain begins engagement, he forces open one hesitant and heavy eye as he raises his throbbing head, just the slightest of distances, from the horizontal, only to be confronted by two tar-dark circles not far from his nose.

Eyes, he calculates, as fast as reasonably possible; the outline of a nose aiding his muddled thinking. These are deep-set eyes though, and as dark as the contents of the barrels of pitch that once lined the quayside, over at Tar Point, all ready to caulk the ships of His Majesty's fleet that once laid at anchor there.

Eyes yes, they are most definitely eyes, even Johnny's able to record. But what eyes. To Johnny's way of thinking these eyes emit neither colour nor light. Rather, these are eyes that suck all in. They're more akin to black and bottomless holes. Johnny's mind sees them as pools of dark that can only lead directly into Hell itself. (Johnny is of artistic bent, remember).

These are eyes that hold and mesmerise him with the sheer depth of their blackness, a blackness beyond any shade that Johnny can mix and as an artist Johnny's good at blending colours. These eyes, though, are of only the purest black. They grip and control him, hold lord over him. They hold a sway as he stares into them whilst the eyes themselves give away nothing.

Johnny's paramount thought is to stay prone, wherever he is, whatever he's lying on. He truly can't remember, for the moment, but these eyes are drawing him, black and inhuman as they are. Johnny, against his own, better judgement, stirs further still, in an attempt to be even the slightest bit more upright.

As the brain stirs, and more cells begin to join the party, Johnny's first frantic feelings of terror begin to fade. The panic subsides as the realisation dawns that the needles in his chest are Bastet's highly sharpened claws, the smell of fish, the odours of Bastet's breath as she purrs into his face and that same purring, the steady rhythmic hum he's been hearing.

"Bugger off, Bastet! You evil sod," he mumbles, barely able to part his parched-stiff lips in speech, whilst wafting an ineffectual hand, partially raised and aimed vaguely in the direction of the undeterred cat.

"Just leave me be. Leave me…" His pitiful voice trails off. Lacking the energy to move the moggy from his now half shirted chest, Johnny groans with the headache that's formed and a throat that's hardened to leather.

He slumps back, once more, the short distance to the unforgiving wood. Johnny fades again into his unquiet sleep where now, soulless, black eyes will haunt the remainder of his disappearing night as well as his waking day yet to come.

As a final effort at coherence and command, he mumbles, "Just leave me be." The words, barely audible, struggle to leave his mouth.

The Cat just treads and purrs.

# Early Morning

Day starts at a variety of times for the villagers of Treddoch, dependent as much on their fancy it seems as their particular occupation.

The fact that this is Solstice, summer at its very peak, doesn't confuse them. They are all creatures of pretty much set routine. The sun may already be gaining height, the gulls may have begun to squawk, lost ducklings may be calling for their mindless mother who's already sailing down the river without noticing her missing brood, but it is still early. Only those who need to be or want to be abroad are abroad.

Amongst the earliest of regular risers are the two Nancarrow sisters, April and May. April and May are twins of later middle years and Bakers to the village, having inherited the business from their late father who, in turn, inherited it from his father, and so on.

The Nancarrows have made bread on these premises for generations as the overall state of the aged, but still serviceable coal-fired ovens bare testimony to.

Also, the Nancarrow family were, and still are, Church, not Chapel, but it has never been detrimental to business. A good bread, it seems, will overcome most obstacles and over the period that they've been Bakers to Treddoch, the Nancarrow's have raised their recipes to perfection.

The Twins are named after two of Spring's months, the favourite season of their late mother, Violet. Spring was a time, Violet always felt, when she could breathe again, start the new year properly. Violet had never accepted January the first as its beginning. That was still Winter as far as she was concerned, and the depths of it too.

Violet had always struggled with winter even from a little girl. In fact, over the years, she grew to positively hate it, for the village centre is always cold and dark at this time, the air perpetually smells of the damp that pervades it. The sun's so low in the sky it just doesn't have the energy to raise its head above the surrounding hills.

Violet would have hibernated had it been at all possible.

The birth of the twins had been quite symbolic, at least to Violet, a woman embedded with a certain degree of superstition, for they were born either side of midnight on the last day of April and the first day of May. So, without any hesitation on Violet's part, April and May they were named.

It's proven to be a bit of a bonus over time too, for sharing everything as they do, it's enabled The Twins to enjoy two birthdays each a year!

Reminiscent of two little birds the twins bob about, hardly ever still for a moment, chirping and twittering like sparrows on speed; incessant. All day long they effortlessly flit and hop from task to task with grace and ease taking it turn-in-turn to mix the dough, fill the tins, attend the shop where they wrap and pack, take the cash and keep themselves, and their customers, fully abreast of local gossip.

> If you're ever in Treddoch, and find a need to be *au fait* of local affairs yourself, then do drop into The Bakery for a saffron bun. You'll find it well worth the cost, in more ways than one, and their saffron buns are particularly delicious.

Just to ensure the twins could be told apart, their mother pinned broaches on each of the girls as soon as they went to school. It was a simple solution, daffodil gold for April, blossom white for May and one that works to this day. If you're ever unsure as to which twin is which just check out the brooch. They still wear them.

The Twins were close as girls and have remained close throughout their lives. Much as one might try, no boy was ever able to come between them. Taking one out on a date meant taking the two, an untenable situation in any circumstance for a young man in his prime. Pretty as they were, attention towards them inevitably ebbed as the tide from the harbour; there were easier catches to be made and just as appealing.

Over time The Twins became increasingly used to their own company; thoughts of young men and marriage gradually slipped from view, as boats into a mist. The girls wedded themselves to The Bakery instead. Over time, it's become their secular convent.

The Twins and Old Bill, who helps them with the daily chores of lighting the fire, cleaning the oven and other odd jobs, as may reasonably be required, a phrase that would have appeared in his Contract of Employment had he ever have had one, are, generally, the first to be abroad of a morning.

The yeasting process, like raising the oven to the requisite temperature, takes some considerable time and so an early start's imperative if they're to meet their own imposed deadline of opening at eight-thirty. Even at that hour they usually find they have a small, but steadily growing queue forming outside the door, all eagerly enticed by the smell of fresh, warm bread and the possibility of interesting conversation.

The fact that the baking will continue throughout the morning, right up to lunchtime, in fact, doesn't deter the more eager, anxious as they are to keep abreast of village affairs as much as making a gastronomic purchase.

In village speak, Old Bill's 'a bit simple' but 'a lovely old soul' although of somewhat indeterminate age from just looking at him. Bill's appearance has changed little throughout most of his adult life. He's always looked old, although he must be around the same age as The Twins, perhaps just a shade older, having started work in The Bakery a short while before them.

Totally inoffensive to everyone, Bill's lived a life that's been quiet and generally uneventful. Over the years he's become something of an institution in Treddoch, respected and loved by all. His single, evening pint in the Fishing Loft is always charged at a special rate.

The Nancarrow sisters inherited Bill along with the business, for it was their father who'd taken Bill under his wing when he was just a lad, as bare of education as he was of conversation and, accordingly, generally unemployable. The old Baker had always found enough jobs for Bill to accomplish, without taxing him too much, and Bill achieved them with a good heart, happy to be wanted, pleased to be of use.

Bill arrives at The Bakery door with precision timing every morning. So far, there's never been any exception. He arrives exactly at the moment that the two sisters are descending the outside staircase from their flat above. How he achieves such impeccable accuracy is a mystery to everyone; no one, to this day knows, just how he does it. He just does.

Bill's first job is to tend to the fire, removing its ash and feeding it coal before carrying the sacks of flour from the store to the scales for weighing so that the two Miss Nancarrows don't have to.

Generally speaking, it's also Bill who puts the tins of dough into the oven and takes the piping hot bread out. His last job of the day comes with the end of the final bake when he helps with the scrub and clean.

Bill's, a creature of habit, so he always knows his next task without need of guidance. He also refers to The Twins as 'Miss Nancarrow and Miss Nancarrow', never by their first names. It's something he's always done from the earliest of days and is most likely to, to the end. It's far too late for him to change now.

Treddoch is a small place, hemmed in by hills on either side as it is, so it's quite usual, indeed, almost *de rigeur*, for rumours to abound in such an environ. Abound they do, almost on a daily basis. In Bill's case they are only ever uttered in the most hushed of tones though and never within his hearing, nor that of the twins.

> Bill's father wasn't known at the time of his birth, at least his mother never said who he was, so he'd taken his surname, Pascoe, from her. She was a woman who'd lived her whole life in the nearby hamlet of St Wyllow, a place famous throughout Cornwall for its large Medieval church, named after the saint, and its contrastingly, small congregation, which these days can be mostly accommodated in the front row.
>
> The Hamlet itself lies some partway between Treddoch Harbour and the nearby town.
>
> To this day, Bill's father has never been formally identified though hints and rumours have abounded for a long time. The former Baker, The Twins' father, took center-ground in almost any speculation on the subject.
>
> This was due, in part, to the old Baker's particular fondness for the lad; after all, he'd given the boy a job, hadn't he? Added to which, and perhaps more pertinent,

when looked at in certain lights (though no one has actually defined what these 'lights' are), there are considered to be certain similarities of look between the boy and the old Baker.

As final proof, if further proof was needed, Bill's mother was on the old Baker's country round. It was noted by several that she was always in benefit of the freshest of bread but never, it seemed, ever in receipt of a bill.

Whatever the truth, over the years, Bill, Old Bill, as he has latterly gravitated to, has become something of an institution in Treddoch, a treasure and a treasure is something that's always cared for.

Unbeknown to the rest of the villagers though, the sisters are fully aware of the stories that have circulated about Bill over the years and quite believe them themselves. If not, why else would they have looked after him all this time, just as their father had done? Whichever 'light' you look at him in, there's no doubt, in The Twins' minds, that Old Bill, is indeed their half-brother. Their only wish has been that their mother had never known, though they could never be certain. Violet was an astute woman.

Other than's already been said of the Nancarrow Twins there's little more to tell that's likely to be of interest to the passing day tripper. They're generally kind of heart and sound of business, though perhaps lacking in some of the subtleties of the contemporary concept of customer service. That concept's just as alien to them as that of a 'contract of employment'.

When the time had come, they'd taken over the bakery as if it were their duty. As far as they were concerned, the village must always have a bakery and that task has fallen to their family for generations past.

There does seem to be one problem though; the future. The fact that neither of The Twins has ever married, nor been inclined to the tendencies of their father, is posing a problem. As far as succession planning is concerned it's a problem to which, as we visit today, they've still no solution.

Having no husbands, they have no children and no children, means no heirs. What is to become of The Bakery in the future and with it the village they sometimes wonder. Is this to be one more service lost to Treddoch forever; another one to become little more than photographs in the local museum? They suspect most probably.

There are relations, of course, as might be expected in such a close-knit community, but so far, none of them nor any of their offspring, have shown any interest in the business other than the fact they all expect to share in the inheritance when The Twins have finally baked their last loaf.

Little do any of them realise that the sisters have already made their wills. They stipulate that, on the death of the remaining twin, apart from provision having been made for Old Bill, all assets are to be realised and the monies donated to the Life Boat for reasons still not clear, other than they feel it a worthy cause. To The Twins' minds, it's certainly a more worthy cause than their relatives.

As they sit in their chairs of an evening, side by identical side, they giggle girlish glee as they imagine the faces of their relatives on receiving the news and some of the more lurid comments that are likely to be made.

The Twins may be single and elderly but can't ever be considered prudish!

As the first of the morning's bake is slid into the oven, not far away, in the flat over The General Store, Mr. Enys is putting his arthritic, right foot out of bed. Mrs. Enys does similar with her left foot on the opposite side. It's her job to make the tea and organise breakfast whilst her husband shaves and washes. Mr. Enys is the first of the two to go on duty though his wife will soon be following in his tread.

As businesses go in Treddoch, The Store's pretty well-tuned to the rhythm of village life, opening its doors as the place begins to stir, closing around five o'clock as the pace slackens off and locals and visitors alike begin to think of their evening meals.

The day's bundle of newspapers has been sitting on their doorstep, under the shelter of its porch, from half-past six, waiting to be untied. They're almost as anxious to be taken off the stone-cold floor and put on the racks as the shop's owners are to get them out for sale.

Midsummer or not, today's just another working day for The Store. '*We never close*' should be emblazoned above the doorway as it's the only shop in Treddoch to operate a full seven days a week, fifty-two weeks of the year. Christmas Day is its only exception. It's always been that way. Like the Nancarrow Twins, the Enys's feel they have a duty to the village.

This, perhaps, in part explains why the Enys's never seem to have quite the dreams and longings of their fellow villagers, busy of hand as they always are. There's precious little time to stop and dream for these two. They've also always seemed content with what life's given though. Unlike many of their compatriots, especially the younger ones, the Enys's have never seemed to want for more.

Setting out the newspapers is the first task of the day, without exemption; every day. They know from their years of experience that there'll be readers soon enough, eager for their daily fix of news and Mrs Enys will need to deliver to those houses around and about the shop. Customers have their expectations.

One such is Patience, who lives not many doors away, in Harbour View Cottage. The little house sits alongside the road that starts its rise from the village centre, just outside of the General Store, and heads upwards and away from Treddoch itself, meandering out, by way of the back road, towards St Wyllow.

Much like Mr. Enys, Patience has no need of an alarm. For her, seven o'clock arrives without need of telling. She's had enough of the night by then for Patience no longer has dreams, only memories. Sometimes she wishes she hadn't even those; they can tend to haunt her.

She also has the One-Eyed Dog to think of. He needs to be let into the garden for his first run of the day. Patience is very fond of the dog as he is of her. They give each other mutual comfort, just by dint of their being.

Whilst the dog's out, Patience makes her pot of tea which is ready brewed just as her newspaper plops through the letterbox. The newspaper provides a useful distraction from her thoughts. It also helps Patience keep in touch with the outside world. It's always good, she feels, to see the bigger picture. Living in Treddoch, it's all too easy to become myopic, Patience feels.

Patience sits in her chair, her cup of tea by her side, The One-Eyed Dog at her feet, and reads. Patience is a very placid creature, like the dog; she's one of nature's ladies.

Back in the shop, the delivery bag's already filled ahead of the paper boy's arrival. It needs to be for Mr. Enys has other tasks to attend to soon enough. Customers are already starting to drift in, some with their eyes more open than others. Mr. Enys needs to give them his fullest, if gruffest, of attention.

Some might be happy to stand, content to wait and pay for their purchases in due course but others are in far too much of a hurry to be kept waiting. These are the ones who leave early and return late. Collect and go is their creed as they dash in and straight back out again. They are, for the most part, the ones who work abroad, some travelling as far, each day, as the city itself. They never seem to leave themselves enough time to accomplish everything they've set themselves to do.

"Morning. Thanks. Bye." Notes and coins are offered as papers, cigarettes and other bits and bobs are bought and taken and then, for them, it's off, up and away. There's no time to stop and chat for this crew; its simply "Hi, Bye" and gone, till tomorrow's repeat prescription.

You won't be meeting any of these today; they'll be long gone by the time you arrive. They also won't be returning till long after you've left. That's when the village has quietened down once again after the frenetic activity that the tourist influx brings with it and regains some sense of a normality.

Slowly, as the morning progresses, the number of customers will start to swell. What begins as little more than a trickle just after opening quickly develops into a steady flow, requiring both Mr. and Mrs. Enys to serve. This is always a good sign, for the till is as eager as the customers, it seems, to be fed.

Life also begins to stir in one of the several restaurants that now stretch the length and breadth of the village. It's The Captain's Table, appropriately re-named, owned as it now is by a former seafarer of vast adventures and global personal proportions, The Captain, in conjunction with, his petite, blonde and land-hugging wife.

The restaurant is traditional in both character and cuisine; lobster, a speciality, is proclaimed proudly on a board beside the entrance. The building itself nestles, as it has done, from the day when it was a new-build, four centuries past, to the eastern side of the harbour, forever facing the elements. Although it does so with a casual disdain a fresh coat of paint is considered desirable each spring, if only to entice would-be diners through the low hanging doorway, with its 'mind your head sign', usually spotted just that tad too late!

The Captain and his wife live in, what might, at a cursory glance, be thought of as a conventional flat above the restaurant, and so, for the most part, it is. There's a lounge, kitchen, three bedrooms and bathroom, the usual stuff of estate agency brochures. The part that isn't quite so usual though is a small snug off the lounge which the Captain insists on claiming to be his 'Cabin'. It's a throw-back to his wondrous days at sea and, more practically, an escape pod, a hidey-hole, his personal panic room from a house filled with women, as fond though as he is of them all.

> The Cabin is an Inner Sanctum for The Captain to hide in, away from the clickety-clack of knitting needle conversation, of the three women though there's probably more point, at times he feels, to the needles.
>
> To The Captain's mind there's a continual and incessant jabbering on the subjects of clothes and make-up and of boys. Just when he thinks it might be finished, no, there's still more talk on the same subjects in general and boys in particular.
>
> In The Captain's partial and particular opinion these boys

that seem to have captured his daughters' attentions are the spotty ones, barely into puberty, let alone out of it, gleaned from the pages of popular magazines. The Captain has strong opinions on many things and, spotty youths aside, considers the production of such media to be a waste of good trees.

The Captain's Wife, herself not indisposed to a passing smile towards these younger males when browsing one of her daughters' aforementioned magazines, assures The Captain that it's all transient; a passing phase. When their time to settle comes, The Captain's Wife's assures him, the girls will seek out partners as steadfast and certain as their father.

She tells him that it's all just the result of youthful and over-active glands and pats his breastbone, reassuringly. This intended calming gesture doesn't reassure The Captain, unfortunately, not as it's intended to. He remembers, with a fair degree of smiling affection, their mother and her glands.

The Captain, aware (his opinion again) of the capricious nature of the female sex, is not so certain, and maintains his forebodings, despite the continuing reassurances of his more sensible wife. A stalemate in opinion has ensued for these past few months with the Captain, like any good father, continuing to worry for his daughters and The Captain's Wife, like any sensible wife, just getting on with life.

To enhance the maleness of its status and thus deter female predators further, the Cabin Room is decorated with nautical memorabilia to such a degree that his wife refuses to clean in there, house proud as she might be. The Captain records this as a success.

Her view is as practical as it is simple, "Your domain, your clutter, your problem." Otherwise, The Captain's Wife keeps a tidy house and, for his part, The Captain keeps a tidy Cabin, just as in his days afloat.

The Captain, still with a full head of dark hair and appropriately whiskered as befits his rank, rises promptly as ever, summer, winter, rain or shine. Seasons and weathers make no difference to his scheduling; The Captain's rarely blown off course.

He's also a man of flawless routine. He's up and quietly out of bed at six, his first cup of tea brewed by ten past and then showered and dressed, shaving not required, by six-thirty. Breakfast's over by seven with the crockery all washed and stashed, ship-shape fashion. If you didn't know better, you might think he'd never been; there's no sign of any disturbance.

Come seven-thirty it's out the door to stroll, sailor style, to the outer quay where he can stare at horizons far distant. He remembers voyages long past and gulps in lung-fulls of sea infused air before returning, fully satiated, to his now landlocked, dry berthed boat and prepares contentedly once more for the coming day.

His wife who is, by now, up and dressed herself, is ready, as she always was, to greet her sailor husband home, even from such a short voyage.

His two daughters, by contrast and custom, still cling feverishly to their bedding and hide under their eider. Only their noses protrude, like snorkels. Like most in their age group, they're determined to deter day's arrival to the last.

The Captain's a local boy whose birth name, if anyone can remember, he's now been called The Captain for so long, even before he actually was one, is Anthony (Tony) Polglaze. He was born and bred in Treddoch but always, from early days, was impatient to leave its confines and explore the world.

Explore he did, much to his mother's sorrow at the time, for he was her only son. To her mind, and, remember, she was one of a breed of women who barely left the village in her young days, The Captain had not only gone a-roaming but had done so to a world away.

Filled with an unrestrained yearning for adventures The Captain took to wandering not long after leaving school. He joined the merchant navy much like Tom Penhale had done before him, though a generation later, being born a little after The War as he was. Unlike Tom though, who'd gone to sea out of a sense of duty, The Captain had gone willingly, wantonly and remained there for a fair portion of his adult life, wandering, a long time restless, from port to not always exotic port, never settled.

Over time there's been a white girl here, a brown girl there. There were also, Chinese, Vietnamese, Japanese, American, French, whatever; The Captain wasn't fussy in those days. The one consistency though, in whatever sea he found himself, it was never the same girl twice.

For Tom, on the other hand, when the time came and the task accomplished, he couldn't wait but return to the safe haven of Treddoch Harbour, his harbour, and the comforting arms of his one love, his Mary.

Somewhere though, in the North Sea, The Captain's roaming habit unwittingly changed. He met and married a Dutch girl, a woman of good taste and impeccable English, which she spoke with an adorable accent. She captivated The Captain. She was the first and only girl he ever saw more than once. To this day he's never understood why, just happy that he did so.

They have two daughters both with bright blue eyes and natural blonde hair. Fortunately for them they tend to favour their mother in looks.

The two had met in Rotterdam, where The Captain's new ship was berthed. He'd bumped into her, The Wife-To-Be, quite literally in the market there. He'd bowled her over, in fact.

They were both walking through the market in the large square, near to the Old Harbour at the time; The Captain never could keep very far away from water. He was looking upwards as he walked, amazed at the sight of the Cube Houses there. Being a practical man, he failed to see their supposed resemblance to a tree, let alone a forest.

To The Captain, a man of oil and engines, of instruments and more earthly matters, anyone with an artistic bent occupied another plain altogether in his mind. It was one far removed from his, one he never could nor ever would understand. It was also one he would never wish to.

Exactly at the same time as The Captain was looking up at the houses The-Wife-To-Be, as familiar with the Cubes as her own face in her morning mirror, found more interest in the stalls she was passing. With her head at nearly ninety degrees to her body, though walking straight, eyes grazing the loaded stalls rather than the course she was following, it was inevitable; CRASH!

He apologised, profusely.

She accepted, demurely.

"Are you alright?" He was mortified he may have hurt her, a woman of so slight a figure she seemed.

"I'm fine, thank you. No harm done," she replied graciously. She was, in fact, a woman built of much hardier substance than her lightweight frame suggested. "It was as much my fault," she continued, eager for him not to shoulder all the blame.

It was all very dignified.

Could he offer her a coffee? As recompense. Though he was a big chap in stature, The Captain was also nimble of mind.

"Yes please, I'd like that. Thank you." In fact, she liked the offer very much, but this thought she kept to herself; for the now. "Do you know Rotterdam well," she'd asked.

A simple, "No. I've come to join my new ship. We sail in a few days."

"Perhaps I can recommend a café?"

He said she could.

She did.

"I know a nice one, just off the square." The Captain looked a man of taste, she felt. She didn't think he'd favour one of the fast-food outlets that were now so readily abounding. The-Wife-To-Be was right; she'd summed The Captain up from very early on in their relationship and to good effect.

They coffeed as comfortably as two souls might do after a thousand years together. It also helped, perhaps, that her father too was an Old Salt and The-Wife-To-Be had a penchant for the sailor type.

For The Captain's part, The-Wife-To-Be was blonde, a particular weakness of his, and with a Dutch accent and plaited braid hanging down her back to boot he didn't stand a chance. As big a man as The Captain is, The Captain's Wife-To-Be had him floored from the start.

They'd settled in Rotterdam for a while, as it was now The Captain's home port, but the Captain never lost sense of his roots, no matter how much he wandered. He'd always intended to return to Treddoch, his home harbour, one day, when his wanderlust was extinguished.

The Captain's Wife never says whether she misses her family home or not. She's always very clear, whenever asked, home, for her, is where The Captain is.

A dutiful daughter though, she telephones her father each, and every week and undertakes twice yearly trips from furthest west to eastern English coast to board a ferry back to Rotterdam, complete with his granddaughters and son-in-law, all part of her travelling luggage.

The Captain is more than happy to acquiesce and not all due to his fondness for his wife. She's fully aware that such acquiescence is as much to do with the fact that he's able to stand on the deck of a rolling ship once more, although no more than a ferry now. He can scan the horizon, feel the undulating waters under his feet and taste the ozone at the back of his throat as he once did, as much as undertake a dutiful visit his father-in-law.

Through wisdom and time, The Captain's Wife has come to know how to keep The Captain content.

The Captain was always careful with his money from the very earliest of his days. Though, for the most part, he'd lived on distant seas and shores he'd shrewdly bought a cottage in Treddoch Harbour just as soon as income allowed. It was lovingly tended during his long absences by his mother who wished him safe each morning as she woke and each evening as she laid her head.

In between, The Captain's Mother cherished his sporadic letters, keeping everyone in a shoebox on a shelf in her wardrobe. The Captain's cottage gave his mother comfort and the confidence that one day her errant son would return, as return he did, both within her lifetime and with the bonus of a daughter-in-law and two granddaughters.

The purchase proved a wise investment too, as property values have risen by extravagant proportions throughout the village over the years and The Captain and his Wife have ploughed the proceeds from its recent sale into their current culinary venture, 'The Captain's Table'.

The property was already an existing eatery when The Captain and his Wife bought it, advertising locally caught lobster and crab, fresh daily, as a speciality. Previously and unimaginatively, it was called the 'Harbour Restaurant' although, in fairness to its former proprietor, the naming quite adequately explained both location and function.

The Captain feels that the renaming, together with improved furnishings, has helped raise the tone of the establishment though and, with that, the prices he can charge.

Buy the time The Captain's on his stroll, he's not the only one to be out and about. Treddoch's starting to come to life, albeit quietly. People seem to walk with a softness at this hour though and if they talk it's always in quieter tones. No-one as yet, feels they want to disturb the day; it'll be disturbed soon enough.

Tom Penhale and John Tregear are such a two. They're now old fishermen, who've long-since hauled their last fish but, through custom and practice, are used to being out and about, looking at the tides as if they're still waiting for one. They're unable to stay within the confine of their walls for very long, always ready and restless as they are to be out for their first wander of the day, around the harbour. They usually meet up somewhere along the quay and, inevitably, discuss old times as men, their age, are wont to do.

"Morning Captain," they greet as he passes; passes but never stops. The Captain always has other business on his mind and, as yet, is far too young to be standing long hours, recollecting times now gone.

He's also anxious to get to the sea's edge for his daily fix. Its ozone is The Captain's cocaine.

"Morning gentlemen. Fine morning. The glass is up. Looks set for fair weather ahead," he comments, barely breaking stride.

The two old fishermen nod and can't help but agree though Tom's sensing something of a front moving in.

Rose Cottage stands on the opposite side of the little river that bisects the village to The Captain's Table and is somewhat further inland.

To the accidental tourist who stumbles across it, the place is the very epitome of everything everyone believes an English cottage should look like. It's a place to swoon over, particularly for the metropolitan mind.

As if it's not enough that the building's all so charmingly higgledy-piggledy in structure, its porch-framed door's festooned at this time of year with a rambling of red roses and the little patch that serves as a front garden is profuse with a, seemingly, random planting of cottage flowers, all accentuating the effect to perfection.

Standing there, outside of its little wrought iron gate it's hard, with just a casual glance, to imagine how the owner's managed to cram so many plants, daisies, foxgloves, carnations, sweet williams, peonies, campanulas and her particular favourite, a lavender bush, all into such a tiny strip. But cram she has and all to such worthy effect. Although it may be small, this little patch has been of great comfort and solace to her over the years, more than its diminutive size might suggest and far better than any prescribed medication could ever have been.

At Rose Cottage, as we visit this morning, the 'Bed & Breakfast' sign that hangs out front is accompanied by another one, proudly announcing the cottage to be 'Full'. Louise, the owner, a woman widowed young, is up and bustling, preparing for the 'breakfast' part of the offering though with just a bit more of a spring in her step than usual. Louise has also taken to smiling a lot more than she was previously used to, particularly to herself it's been noticed. Questions are being asked, though never directly. So far, even The Bakery's not been able to supply an answer.

Louise, now in her mid-forties, has a man in her life once more, something she'd all but given up hope of ever believing would happen again. Under the circumstances, she's quite happy to forget that Robert is some ten years younger than herself as well as someone prone to flitting from woman to woman as much as around the world with his work as he does. Robert seems to be the sort destined to be forever single.

In his defence, Robert has always declared that he's not promiscuous, it's just that he hasn't found the right woman yet. Louise daren't hope that she could be that woman. No one else has been so far, not even her two daughters in their time.

Louise had married young. She was eighteen and pregnant with her first child Samantha, Sam. Her husband, Bertram, a tall, willow of a man was the youngest son of members of the upper-middle classes. Unlike his two brothers though Bertram, Bertie, had more Bohemian tendencies. Much to his parents' dismay, Bertie didn't follow them into the City.

Instead, Bertie had taken to pottery and at that time the only place to be, as far as Bertram was concerned, was Cornwall and in particular, St. Ives, where he learned his craft. He'd probably have stayed there forever had it not been for Louise, but Treddoch Harbour wasn't a million miles from his spiritual home, and he was happy that Louise had family in the village to help after the baby was born. Bertie acknowledged that he was pretty useless with domestic matters himself but threw a magnificent bowl to commemorate his first daughter's birth.

Bertram's parents had found it difficult, originally, to come to terms with their son's choice of occupation let alone his marriage to someone they considered to be a social inferior, but they were the sort of people who had standards to maintain.

They were also sufficiently well-endowed, financially speaking. Their new granddaughter wasn't going to be born into poverty, at least not into a poverty as they perceived it could be. Rose Cottage was a wedding gift and not only large enough for a young family but also a place with space for Bertie to have his own small studio.

To Louise, a local village girl, she seemed as if she'd everything. By the age of little more than twenty, she'd two daughters, a home of her own and a talented, loving husband. All her Christmases had come together it had seemed at the time. Louise couldn't have been happier nor more content if she'd tried.

Like so many children of her time, Louise had been an enforced church-goer when young and was married in church, although, by then, church was more a matter of custom and habit than it was of faith.

As she grew older, Louise, along with most of her contemporaries, shied away from the church altogether. Religion became an irrelevance, although she still remembered much of her Sunday-school teachings, including the quotation, 'the Lord giveth and the Lord taketh away'. Louise wasn't much inclined to the rest of the quote though, 'Blessed be the name of the Lord' when, after only ten years of marriage, God took her dear, wonderful, loveable Bertie at only thirty-five, from cancer.

As much as comfort for herself, as well as in memory of her beloved Bertie, Louise threw herself into raising their two daughters. Love and her personal gratification weren't even lifted to the level of second place for a long time, not, in fact until Robert has come along.

From the financial perspective, following on from Bertie's death, Louise was fortunate; she wasn't in dire financial straits by any means. The in-laws had seen to that, if only for the sake of their grand-daughters. Louise did, however, need something to occupy herself with other than the two girls and so took to running the cottage as a small bed and breakfast business. The additional cash was a bonus.

Robert first came into Louise's life eight years ago when the two girls Sam, then twenty and Ellie, eighteen were still at home. Robert was just getting over the emotions of his first break-up and had decided on a holiday in Cornwall. By the purest of chances, he'd stumbled into Treddoch Harbour that first night and in particular, through Louise's door where he'd taken a room, initially, just for the night. He finally returned to London and a new job some three months later as his funds ran low.

In the meantime, Robert had had a wonderful summer with the two girls who'd shared him quite amicably between themselves. Louise, in some ways more of an elder sister than a mother to the girls, had taken quite a fancy to Robert herself but, with her daughters as competition, had never stood a chance; not that she'd tried. She had envied the girls though.

Robert had kept in touch with them all for a while but a stint abroad and a new relationship put an end to that as he'd moved all those airline miles away. None of them had heard from him in a long time. Suddenly, a couple of weeks ago and eight years on from that summer, Robert was back in Britain and single once again. He'd decided on a short break before starting his new job and, for no particular reason, and from out of nowhere, had thought of Cornwall and that summer long past.

He'd headed south-west once more, fingers crossed, in the hope that Louise might still be running her bed and breakfast and of course, that the girls might still be around. Louise was but the girls weren't. The evening itself had turned into something of a bittersweet reunion.

On seeing Robert standing there, in the open doorway, Louise's mouth had dropped open in disbelief for a second before turning to a broad smile.

"Robert? Robert? It is you, isn't it?"

"Who else?" he'd said, as Louise threw her arms around him, giving him a kiss and a hug.

"How wonderful to see you again. What a lovely surprise after all this time. Come in, come in," and she positively dragged him through the door and into the little hallway.

"Are you staying? How long?" all part of a string of questions which Robert struggled to answer in time before the next one hit him. Finally, "throw your bag down there," she'd said, pointing to a spot in the corner.

Robert explained that he was single again, to which Louise shook her head, smiling, and on a week's holiday. He'd said he'd thought it'd be great to see her and, of course the girls, if they were around.

No, they weren't, but she'd explain later.

Robert had also said that he'd hoped Louise might have had a room, for a day or two, perhaps, the week if possible.

No luck there, either, the 'Full' sign, attached to the 'Bed & Breakfast' one was correct.

"All the rooms are taken I'm afraid," she'd said and then, putting her hand to the top of his arm and giving it a little squeeze continued, "but don't worry, we can sort something out, later I'm sure." With that, she dismissed the problem. Robert didn't question it.

"Come on through," and she'd led him into the lounge, producing a bottle of wine and two glasses along the way, as they settled on the sofa to reminisce.

Louise explained that Sam was now married and living with her solicitor husband, two-point-four children, a rescued mongrel dog, a cat that bossed the dog and a sensible estate car, on the outskirts of Truro.

Then came the bitter part of the evening for, inevitably, Robert had also asked after Ellie, the daughter that had favoured her father both in her looks and eccentricity.

Ellie, Louise had explained had been dead the past four years. It had happened in London. She'd been killed by a drunk driver, a trader in the City. It seems that he'd been celebrating some deal he'd just completed. Ellie was heading home after working late, walking the last bit. She always liked to get some exercise having been sat at a desk all day.

"She's buried, in the cemetery here; he's walking free now, somewhere," Louise had said, with a note of resentment, adding, "Now I've lost the two of them, Bertie and Ellie," for whilst Ellie was alive, so was Bertie to Louise.

Louise had taken a larger than average slurp of wine to wash away her sadness. Then, brightening a little, she'd added, "still, looking on the bright side, Sam's named her daughter Ellie, in memory, so I have something."

Shaking off her sadness, Louise had moved her glass into her left hand and had relaxed back into the settee once more. She'd pressed up somewhat closer to Robert as well. With her eyes wide and bright and smiling once again, she turned to face him, running her right hand softly along his thigh. "I know the cottage's full tonight," she'd said, "but there's always space in my room. If you want, that is. You're very welcome to share."

It had all been a bit of a gamble, helped by the wine, but Robert had stayed, and for the week. It was strange, having someone to snuggle against again. Louise only hoped that Bertie understood.

That was all of two weeks ago and Robert has, so far, 'phoned Louise every night as promised; hence the almost silly smile that's been hanging around her face of late. Not only has Robert 'phoned as promised, he's also visiting in a couple of days for a long weekend.

Louise, as excited as a sixteen-year-old with the prospect, was tempted to close the business for the period but Robert, quite firmly, had said 'no'. Business was business; Louise would need the money. He'd fit in around Louise and her schedule.

If there was ever a way of getting bonus points Robert had bagged a hatful.

Of all the sights and sounds that may have been seen and heard this morning though, one, sadly, to some way of thinking, is missing. The one sound you'll no longer hear anymore in these early, Treddoch hours is the steady clanking of bottles. Neither will you hear the consistent creaking of gates nor treading of feet for The Milkman, has become extinct in Treddoch Harbour, wiped out by the general move to plastic milk.

Even The General Store, that bastion of the traditional with its old-fashioned mechanical till, has, for once, followed with the trend. The crate of bottles that once stood just inside the door no longer does. Milk is now to be found in colour-coded containers, of varying sizes, on temperature-controlled shelves; all very initiative for Mr. and Mrs. Enys.

The Milkman and his bottles are another piece of Treddoch's past, consigned to history and the local museum.

# Nine O'Clock, or Thereabouts

Nine o'clock is, in many ways, *the* most pivotal time of the village's day, particularly weekdays. It is, in general terms, that point at which it can be said, with a fair degree of certainty, that Treddoch Harbour is most definitely alive and awake after the previous night. There's a positive noise and a bustle about the place; a steady hum.

Just about everyone's up and dressed by now, with the probable exception of Rockabilly Joe. Nine o'clock's a trifle early for Rockabilly; he's something of a night-bird.

It all harkens back to his band days when Rockabilly rocked all night and lay stupefied for most of the day. You'll need to wait till a while later to meet with him, nearer lunchtime in fact, but don't worry, we're here most of the day.

Breakfasts are, in general finished, although, in their house on the cliffs, on a small development to the eastern side of the village, Joan and Henry are still sitting, sipping cups of double espresso. A double expresso after breakfast is another of Joan's more recent fads. Left to himself Henry would much prefer a good, large mug of instant but, like so many things, that's something else that Henry's had surgically removed from his life since his new relationship.

Joan is also looking at holiday brochures which, to Henry's mind, are proving to be of the more expensive variety, although Joan prefers to refer to them as, 'the more exclusive'.

Whichever way it's put, Henry's convinced it all comes back to the same thing. He's going to have to dig deep, which partly explains why he's mining the financial pages of his newspaper this morning and wondering just how much more of a beating his investments are going to have to take.

Henry used to be pretty risk-averse as far as investing's concerned, but since Joan came on board, he's had to take an increasingly more active position. Joan may watch her food intake, but she has a large, financial appetite.

∞

All the traditional village shops are open now, and the streets are beginning to fill. It might seem to be slow, at first, but the momentum will, without exception, gather pace as people meander from each and every which way towards the shops, towards their places of work, towards the surgery, towards the school, towards wherever and then, inevitably, back again.

Whether in a scurry or in a stroll their paths can't help but crisscross in such a confined space as the village centre occupies, and time has to be taken to pass pleasantries, even if for just the briefest of seconds, as the one passes the other. Anything but would be considered rude in such a tight-knit community as Treddoch Harbour where, historically at least, everybody was just about related to everybody else, one way or another.

As some speak merely in the passing, others come to a complete stop. Groups start to collect as people grind to a halt. Small clusters accumulate at random points as villagers, content to share the moment for a while, begin to engage in early morning conversations.

Suppliers vehicles too are starting to arrive, all eager to drop their deliveries and begone as quickly as possible. Treddoch's not a place they relish delivering to. Some, more properly, do use the car park provided, but others are determined to park as close to their destinations as possible, narrowing further already narrow roads, bringing varying degrees of their own brand of chaos in their wake. The children, on their way to school, bring another.

∞

A little before eight-thirty, during term time, the Long Trek begins although this one's somewhat more disorderly even than the original. In fact, if anything, this Trek is more of a Melee really.

Parents, mothers generally, though not exclusively, there are one or two fathers thrown into the mix, gather slowly at various points along the route, shepherding the younger children, from the harbour end towards the primary school. The gathering increases in numbers *en route* as the caravan rolls forward, somewhat akin to a snowball growing ever bigger as it moves, until, reaching critical mass, it becomes unstoppable.

There's the usual repertoire of greetings, regurgitated each, and every morning, just as if the participants haven't seen each other for years, rather than only the day previous and all starting with,

"Morning Jane."

"Morning Jean."

"Morning John."

"Morning all." Sometimes it's just easier to give a generic greeting; it can save a lot of effort, particularly at that time of the morning. It's still relatively early, remember; the caffeine's barely had time to take hold.

From such little beginnings though, conversations develop, grow, enlarge and multiply, becoming subjects in their own right, acquiring lives of their own, all of which require the group or sub-groups to grind to a halt at several points in the Trek. In these moments, issues are discussed, opinions passed, gossip traded, lives dissected.

What should be a relatively short journey by any account is turned into a long haul for no other reasons than these. It's been calculated that it can be quicker to commute in the city than at peak times in Treddoch, but then, no one has time for anybody else in the city. It's all 'heads down' there; scurry on. That's not the village way where there's nearly always time for a conversation of some sort with someone or other. The morning walk to school provides the perfect opportunity.

Herding cats might seem easier, to the casual visitor, as parents and children drift in ill-defined groups spanning the breadth of the road. There's no clear leadership, no coherent strategy, no co-ordinated policy within the group so it's not easy to usher them, for instance, all to the same side of the road, when a vehicle approaches.

At these moments, parents have a propensity to deliver opposing instructions, so children dart from side to side seeking refuge until finally and dramatically they pin themselves to the walls of the houses that line the route. It's quite usual, in fact, for them to end, some on each side, narrowing the road space even further, making life that little more difficult for the approaching driver. Even Job's patience would be tested.

Vehicle passed, the children peel themselves from the walls and the Melee reforms, moving inexorably onwards towards the school gates, now formally opened by The Caretaker, a man who's held the post since time immemorial.

The Caretaker particularly enjoys this time of his day, seeing the younger children, watching them grow and move up, as they must, through the school. He's known them all over time, some now with children of their own.

On mornings like today, he's minded to think of his own son, and the grandson he's never seen, only heard of second-hand.

There was an altercation, some five years back. Bitter words were said between father and son, the sort of words which once spoken are difficult to retract, particularly for two individuals as intractable as those two are. They're as stubborn as each other, The Caretaker's Wife says.

The boy packed his belongings, took his car, crossed to somewhere beyond the Tamar and has never contacted his father since although he has his mother, which is how The Caretaker knows about the grandson that's little more than hearsay to him. There are also a couple of photographs on the sideboard which he's prone to look at when his wife's not around.

The Caretaker's Wife has never forgiven the old man for his part in the altercation but he's stubborn and age isn't softening him. He remains intransigent, holding on to the firm belief in the rightness of his position in the argument. So far, nothing's been able to shift his stance and as time continues its progression, it seems there'll be nothing that will unless, of course, it's this coming Christmas. It'll be interesting to see if Christmas is likely to make any difference.

As far away as Christmas yet is, The Caretaker's Wife has already stated that this year, come what may, she will be staying with their son and his family. It's already arranged. The Caretaker can do as he pleases though he's welcome to come. If he stays home, though, it's up to him but he needn't expect her to leave everything organised for him. He was told that quite emphatically and The Caretaker's Wife is prepared to be as stubborn as the old man in this regard.

He'll have to 'sort himself out', as his wife bluntly put it, which will be interesting to watch, given that The Caretaker's the sort of man who can barely boil an egg.

Amazingly and seemingly against all the odds, somehow, parents and children all manage to arrive at the school gates in time for the start of lessons. Little ones are kissed and waved to as they run off in one direction whilst their elders turn and walk back in the other. Shopping, work, social visits all begin to beckon.

Another day in Treddoch is fully underway.

May Nancarrow, at The Bakery, has already opened the doors to the assembled gathering that was waiting dutifully outside and welcomed both them and their purses in.

The General Store is in full swing as returning parents help swell the happy band of shoppers washing steadily in and out, purchasing for the day ahead.

Jack, in the butcher's shop, Tamsyn's butcher's shop that is, has his window all laid out with the freshest of cuts. He's taking the hiatus between the preparing and the selling to grab an early cup of tea and have another ponder on the meaning of life; at least that part that's his.

With her Little Ones having been put on deposit for the day, Lizzy, along with several of the now dispersing throng of parents, turns villagewards herself, food shopping being her next domestic.

Lizzy's first stop, as of habit, is with The Butcher. It really doesn't seem so long ago she's inclined to think that it was

Butcher Trelawney standing there, apron-clad, cleaver in hand, round of middle, smiling towards her through the plate glass of his shop as she approached. It must be getting on for two years come this Autumn she recollects.

Lizzy can still picture him, behind his block, though the picture's already beginning to haze around the edges. One day, and it won't be that long in coming, his image will have faded altogether; an outline she can no longer quite put features to.

Now though it's Jack that's standing there, not that Lizzy seems to mind the change. In fact, Lizzy seems to rather prefer it, but puts that down to no more than the fact that she's known Jack since childhood rather than anything else.

The three of them, Lizzy, Tamsyn, and Jack had all been in the same year at school. Lizzy had had a school-girl crush on Jack, she remembers, but that was a long time ago. She shakes her head to clear the fog of fond reminiscence, declining to admit to herself that she still seems to have a too soft a spot for him and rather enjoys her daily visit to his shop. To Lizzy's mind, the butcher's shop is Jack's, and nobody else's.

Lizzy could never become vegetarian she realises. Cutting out meat would mean cutting out her morning visits to Jack; far too vegan a process for Lizzy to contemplate.

Jack looks forward to Lizzy's visits with an equal enthusiasm. Perhaps, like Lizzy, it's due to a memory shared from the past or maybe it's just that Lizzy always crosses the threshold with a bounce in her step, warmth in her face and with eyes bright and clear. There's always an exuberant greeting of 'Morning Jack' which he holds as defence against the icy draught that's all too soon to come when Tamsyn enters for the day, at least for that part of the day before the afternoon clean-up has to be started.

At that point Tamsyn, like her mother before her, excuses herself. Surprisingly, she always has something else to do, back at home, to where she makes a hasty retreat. Tamsyn never admits that it's to have a sleep; tiredness catches up with her by mid-afternoon. Worrying about her money Tamsyn finds very wearing; it keeps her awake much of the night.

Lizzy, in contrast, bursts into the Butcher's shop of a morning, olive of eye, bronze of summer thigh, skin as flawless as a Shakesperean metaphor and with a countenance as bright and bubbly as a fresh Champagne. It's a perfect vision for a man locked in a loveless marriage.

'Fizzy Lizzy', is how Jack likes to think of her. It's not that Jack actually knows that much about Champagne though; Tamsyn's domestic budget doesn't allow for it. A nightly glass of malt is Jack's allowance, and he's made to feel that he should be grateful for that.

Although allowing it, Tamsyn doesn't really approve of the whisky. Her father certainly never had one, nor did her Granfer but then, Jack's not really Chapel. He's hardly even Church, if it comes to it.

Lizzy's childhood crush on Jack had been reciprocated initially, but having taken a job with Butcher Trelawney, on leaving school, Jack had somehow strayed his earlier path and walked another for little more than a roof over his head, fire in a winter's hearth and a rib of beef on Sunday.

Where's the love that should be, he's started to wonder, particularly as he minces the beef fresh each morning; his first job of the day. The early quiet of the morning, with just some carcasses and his thoughts as companion, provides Jack with another opportunity for pondering. So far, though, none of these ponderings have been very helpful. Instead of providing answers they're just causing him more confusion, especially when Lizzy bounces in.

Lizzy, a modern girl in most ways, enjoys a shorter length of skirt in her limited wardrobe. She has the legs for it. Jack rather likes them, the legs and the hemline. Tamsyn, in contrast, favours a hemline somewhere below the knee; she doesn't have the legs for the shorter length. She doesn't have the curves either. Jack's recently started to notice the curves on Lizzy and can only sigh, both for what he does have as much as what he doesn't.

Tamsyn always thinks of herself as slim; Lizzy regards her as skinny. She tends to believe that her more ample figure offers more for a man to get hold of.

For her part, Tamsyn's not all that keen on having any bits of her, 'gotten hold of'. Even Jack's attentions are kept to a dutiful level.

"One up on you, Tamsyn Trelawney and all your money," resorting to Tamsyn's maiden name, Lizzy mentally comments as she smirks to herself, "with your Lowry white sticks. No wonder you wear your skirts so long."

Such a statement's an unusual and uneven outburst of temperament for Lizzy, but then, nobody's completely perfect this side of celluloid, although Jack, of recent times, has begun to think that Lizzy might be and Tamsyn and Lizzy are now as much apart as they had once been close.

The Thought is also possibly induced by a lingering fondness for Jack, leftover from that long-ago time. "Why did you let yourself be seduced for little more than a string of sausages Jack? Was it worth it?" Lizzy wonders, as she pays for her purchase, smiling somewhat pityingly at him.

Jack, desperate not to be thought in any way perverted, focuses intently on Lizzy's face as she crosses the threshold, concentrating twice as hard as necessary on her meat order, maintaining eye contact, at all times. It's much the best solution, in the circumstances, he feels although Lizzy's smile is just as unnerving for a chap on meagre rations.

Unbeknown to Jack, Lizzy has noticed him admiring her legs and, surprised as she is, she finds that she quite likes it. Lizzy's rather proud of her legs and appreciates the attention, having no one at home to give her any. Whilst not admitting it, she's particularly liking the attention coming from Jack.

Unlike some of her fellow villagers, Lizzy is, overall content with what she has. Yes, she would like a home of her own, perhaps a few more clothes but, in the great scheme of things, she's generally satisfied. After all, she has the Little People, at the moment barely big enough to peer over the edge of the kitchen table but growing none-the-less, and a generally care-free life. It's especially so this solstice day. Living under such an azure and tranquil sky and in a place like Treddoch Harbour, Lizzy feels she could want for little more.

It all begs the gnawing question, though, somewhere at the back of her mind, wonderful as she finds them, are the Little People alone, really sufficient to completely fill Lizzy's life. Is she just pretending to herself? Lizzy always tries to affirm that they are enough and that she doesn't need anybody else; that she's quite content. But is she being honest with herself? Even she's beginning to sense that, maybe, there is something missing after all.

Lizzy's mother would certainly question it, though, as in most things with regards to her daughter, Lizzy's mother keeps her own counsel. After all, Lizzy's still a young woman, fully in her prime, as Jack would readily testify if pressed.

Although Jack's neither Chapel nor Church he still fervently prays, to whatever god that might be listening, that he won't be.

Jason Henley, Pie and Pasty Maker, has been working an hour now, in the quiet, pre-nine period, preparing puff and other pastries together with contents for pies and pasties yet to be baked. By comparison with the Nancarrow Twins his is a sleek and modern operation, for Jason cooks by electricity.

*'No soot and grime to clean each day, just flick a switch and bake away!'* went the advert for the electric oven. Jason believed and bought; he's not been disappointed. So easy and, as a bonus, if anything does go wrong with the oven, he merely calls on the engineer for specialist assistance.

As a further bonus, to Jason's mind, he can arrive at work at a more civilised hour than the Nancarrow Twins too. The electric oven has proven to be ideal for someone with a greater partiality for his mattress, a man whose third love, after his wife and his stomach, is his bed.

Jason would gladly recommend that the Twins convert, to electricity that is, but he knows they'll be too set in their ways. Advice given with the best of intentions may be deemed as unwarranted interference when it's received. Bread has always been baked in coal ovens in Treddoch and as long as there's a Nacarrow at the baking table, then it's most likely that that will always be the way.

With a name such as his, Jason is clearly not a local boy. From the villagers' perspective, he'd come from somewhere 'up north', by which they mean, of course, anywhere east of the Tamar River. However, for geographical expediency it should be noted that Jason hails from Birmingham, though he's long been accepted into the local fabric, mainly because he's kept his head down, his mouth closed and hasn't expressed unwanted opinions on village affairs. These days, Jason's considered to be very much 'local'.

Jason's status has also benefited from the fact that, not long after the departure of the original girlfriend, the one brought with him from Birmingham, Jason had soon taken-up with a local girl from a somewhat extended family spread throughout both the village and surrounding hamlets. They'd all approved him. It had further raised his credentials when, later on, the liaison had turned into marriage, complete with offspring.

Jason had arrived in Treddoch Harbour one early Spring afternoon when he, like the year, was still quite young though he was the greener.

He'd arrived in what had once past been a shiny and proud camper van. By the time it had come into Jason's stewardship though, it was already a sad and pathetic looking heap, dull rust-blue in colour with one windscreen wiper and a front bumper somewhat askew. Its innards were in little better shape, having cost Jason almost more in oil than petrol to complete the trip.

Several rest stops, for the camper's benefit rather than Jason's, were also needed to let the engine cool, though the day wasn't especially hot.

Jason, however, had fallen in love with the van from the day he'd first seen it, more so than with any woman he'd ever known up to that point, so cost and time were unimportant. The imperative was that he and the van reached journey's end together and intact.

Jason was alright but the van only just made it and had to be put into intensive care.

Jason had also arrived that day complete with a waxed and fully expectant surfboard on the roof, a slightly apprehensive girlfriend inside, a Dream in his heart and sporting an earring in one ear. It was, pretty much, the sum total of all that he carried.

It wasn't long though before both the girlfriend and The Dream deserted him though the loss of the girlfriend didn't bother Jason that much, not if he were honest. She'd been great fun in her time it was true, all part of a somewhat hedonistic youth, but she wasn't the keeping kind. She was there more for his lust than his life. She soon faded into the past, returning to somewhere with a faster pace, for she was a city girl at heart. Active, urgent, she was the sort of girl who wanted city sounds, strong sounds, sounds to move to, sounds to move with. Treddoch Harbour has always favoured a steadier, quieter style.

Jason wasn't so sorry about the loss of the girlfriend, but the Dream was a different matter. Its loss vexed him, at least at first. Over the years though, as life has sped on and taken a different tack from its original intent, it's come to feature less and less in Jason's space and time.

Eventually, as reality stepped in, The Dream morphed into little more than wishful thinking, mixed with a hint of nostalgia. It was something that was never going to be realised, particularly when the practicalities of earning a living came into view. Priorities had to be made, including paying a monthly rent on the premises he'd leased, next door but one to Butcher Trelawney.

The loss of The Dream certainly saddened Jason in the beginning. He'd missed it with a greater passion than he'd held for the late, unlamented girlfriend, but the pain had steadily eased with the passing of days and the appearance of a new companion, Sarah who proved to be a suitable and pretty immediate distraction.

These days, the surfboard lurks, though long untouched and unwaxed, in some far corner of both mind and home. It's been so long now since it last saw a wave that it's highly probable it wouldn't remember what it was supposed to do if it did see one. Jason would certainly struggle, especially as he no longer sports the lithesome figure that he once did.

The one constant's been the earring which has remained and remains still.

Jason's new girlfriend and eventual wife, Sarah Pendragon, didn't surf. She didn't 'do' water sports of any description. Sarah couldn't and to this day still can't swim, something which Jason had first thought unusual for someone born and bred in such a water-side location. She'd never been inclined to learn either it appeared, for, to Sarah's mind, the sea was something to be viewed and from a distance at that. It wasn't ever something to be part of.

Sarah has always held a healthy regard for the sea's raw, sometime violent and abrasive power and wisely, to her way of thinking, keeps her distance. The closest Sarah ever gets is to stand on the wall of the outer harbour, safe behind the railing, holding tight to it for extra measure.

She watches the boats, looking no bigger than ducklings on the open water, chugging and spluttering their way out to sea and back to harbour again. She's always glad to see them safe for Sarah has a father and a brother in one of them.

On the whole, Sarah prefers to walk the cliff high paths herself. There she can wander along their thyme and ramson edges, pick the flowers from random tufts of sea pinks, primroses and violets and smile indulgently at the sight of the pink-white petals of dog rose.

She adores the hedges of wild sweet pea and the blossoms of even wilder apple, seeded from the discarded cores of strolling hikers. Sarah, like the plants, feels safe there, far above the water's reach. The sea has always only ever been a backdrop, it's never been a draw.

Sarah's lack of surfing prowess didn't, in any way, diminish her attraction to Jason for she's a sensible woman; 'Sensible Sarah' as her mother's always called her. Sarah's a woman who's determined, disciplined and organised. She's the sort of woman that a man with a

Dream was in dire need of.

From the start, Sarah helped a younger Jason organise his life, prioritising his business. She made life a joy and a pleasure for him for Sarah had soon realised that Jason was a laid-back sort of soul; almost as horizontal as his surfboard might have been had it found water. In fairness to Jason though, he was nowhere near as laid-back as Johnny was to become. Johnny was to set a new benchmark in Treddoch.

Sarah quickly learned that encouraging Jason was much easier all round than trying to goad him to action.

As a further inducement to Jason to fall for Sarah, if ever such was needed, Sarah was, and still is an extremely good cook. It didn't take her long to find Jason's weak spot, his stomach. Long before Jason and Sarah wed themselves, his stomach and her cooking had married well.

Coming from Birmingham, home to the British Balti and a place peppered with takeaways of all imaginings, the one and only thing Jason did miss from home was what had come to be his traditional Friday night.

Friday night for Jason had, for a long time been sacrosanct, the night elevated to almost religious proportions. Friday night was curry night whether eaten out or in. It became a night to be revered. How you made a curry though, Jason had absolutely no idea which didn't help him much in his self-imposed exile in Treddoch where the concept of a takeaway stretched little further than the local fish and chip shop, The Saucy Cod.

Aware that a curry was Jason's particular favourite of any foods, Sarah soon set about the task of cooking one, together with all the trimmings. She reinstated Friday night in Jason's weekly calendar to its former level.

Sarah included a decent beer too, for good measure. Jason was easily won over.

All through the full length of their relationship Sarah has always ensured that there are a couple of iced beers to hand. It's the attention to detail that make the difference she believes.


After catering college and a stint with a traditional baker back home, Jason had dreamed to a point beyond fantasy of opening a similar establishment to the one where he'd learned his trade, but in Treddoch Harbour.

Treddoch had always held a particular space in Jason's heart. It was the place of childhood holidays, a place for which he held only sunshine memories. Treddoch was more than a fishing harbour to Jason. It was a Utopian haven filled with ice creamed and candy flossed dreams, a place, in his mind, where life is one long excursion. There was no gritty reality.

Jason conveniently buried memories of wet days, the ones that had kept him from the beach and tides that had washed away his carefully built sandcastles. He forgot about the salted tears, shed for their loss. He forgot how they'd rolled down his cheeks and plopped, one by one, into the greater salt stream of the insurgent waters, adding that little extra to the oceans' depths. So far had Jason brain-washed himself.

Jason's business plan, using the term at its loosest, was simple. Up early, bread baked and sold by lunchtime, surfing come the afternoon, pub of an evening. Simple to the point of stupidity.

The first problem encountered was that, generally speaking, Jason was on the wrong coast for the surfing, the waves being much better on the northern side.

Secondly, as far as the bakery idea was concerned, he soon came to realise that setting up in competition to the Nancarrow sisters, might not be the most sensible thing to do. Entrenched, as the Nancarrows were, in the very fabric of the community, setting up in competition could prove economic, social and political suicide. Fortunately, Jason's old master had taught him well and on an extensive platform; hence Jason was able to make a swift and immediate shift to a sideways occupation.

Jason has built a sound, successful and steady business over the years but has never done any of his imagined surfing. With two little cost centres to feed and clothe, he has to keep the shop open till six in the Season, seven days a week and then there are the domestics Sarah requires of him at any time of the year.

Occasionally, though, gazing eyeless into a whirlpool of old memories as he mechanically mixes meat and veg in varying assortments in their bowls he might, on occasion, wistfully ask his Dream where it has gone.

"To someone else now, Jason. I went long, long ago. I'm surprised you still remember me. Gone to someone with shorts and board, someone with sun-blonded hair and a more ardent desire to ride the crest. I couldn't wait with you forever. We were never really going anywhere, were we? We were never really an item. Just hung out together for a while, more like bar-room buddies than bosom pals really. Not really, Team Jason, were we?"

Jason can only nod in agreement.

Life isn't that bad though. Business is good, as are the children, on the whole, though they're no angels. They're pretty much like normal children everywhere, for which Jason is at least grateful.

They called the first-born Arthur out of respect for Sarah's grandfather and his unqualified, though persistent, claim that the family was descended not only from Arthur but from Uther Pendragon himself; Uther, the very first of the Pendragon's.

The fact that the concept of Uther's and Arthur's actual existences hang by the merest of threads never deterred the old man in his beliefs and Sarah, dutiful granddaughter, certainly wasn't going to argue against him. Anyway, she liked the name Arthur for its own sake, so Sarah had told herself before she first mooted the idea of the name to Jason. She needn't have worried about Jason's reactions though, Jason's always been more than happy to agree with most things Sarah suggests. After all, they're usually sensible suggestions.

They called the second son Paul, though for no obvious reason.

With both of the children now at school, Sarah's helping in the shop again. It's something Jason particularly enjoys and during school holidays there's a mother-in-law who can usually be dragooned into babysitting assistance for a few hours in the day although Arthur's getting to an age where being supervised by grandma is becoming something of an embarrassment.

Unlike Butcher Trelawney though, Jack has never bought a pie from Jason at five minutes to ten or any other time. Jack chooses a healthier option, an apple. He likes to keep an eye on his weight, apparently, though Jason can't see why for Jack's as thin as the string he uses to tie his meats.

Jason's own figure, in comparison, has grown a little more rounded over the years which he attributes to a comfortable living. He forgets the fact that an overindulgence in his own baking together, with a bottle of beer (maybe two) of an evening and an almost total lack of exercise, are contributing factors.

Exercise, for Jason, is generally confined to a walk between home and work, though he does do it both ways.

Like Jason, Molly too is ensconced at work, first in her office and then her classroom from around eight o'clock. During term time Molly and Jason usually pass each other on the road as Molly hastens 'up' the village to the school and Jason, living at 'the top end' ambles 'down' to his shop. In truth, 'up' and 'down' are academic expressions, given that the village, at this part lies pretty much on level ground.

The school stands at the top end of the village, on the western side of the little river that bisects the place, at the bottom of the hill that leads to the nearby town. It is, by any standards, an easy travel from Molly's cottage by the harbour. Some might think Molly's life idyllic, particularly those whose lives are blighted with interminable commutes each day.

Life, unfortunately, has a tendency to balance itself out. It can take as well as give as Molly can truly attest to. Yes, she saw success at school, gaining good, academic grades which, in turn, propelled her to university, one of the better ones, where she read literature. From there it was a short stint at teacher training college and, eventually, via a fairly rapid career rise, a headship in her home village within walking distance from her cottage on the quay. Add into all this, Molly's still only in her late thirties.

On the downside, as far as Molly's concerned, she's still very single with little apparent opportunity for meeting Mr. Even Almost Right. There are times when Molly would gladly trade all she has for that.

Whilst Lizzy's busy toying with Jack in the Butcher's, over at The Captain's Table, The Captain's descending the creaking wood stairs to the rear, the private ones that connect the flat above to the restaurant below and steadies himself for the day ahead.

This morning's little different to any other morning for The Captain, a man of such set and particular patterns as he is, a man resolute and unwavering of routine. He fills his bucket with hot and soapy water, gathers his brushes and cloths and heads outdoors to face the first of his daily tasks, the scrubbing and cleaning of the front of the premises.

To The Captain's mind, the front of his restaurant is much like the hull of a boat. It's the first part any budding customer sees and as such a probable indicator of what lies inside. It has to be pristine; second-best won't do. Second-best doesn't exist for The Captain; it's not something he's ever settled for.

Brushed and washed, just as The Captain himself, the restaurant now glistens its welcome. There's no longer any litter out front to mar the doorway nor any seagull mess to blight either paint or glass. The windows, once again, gleam clear and bright, perfect for the inquisitive eye to peer through; affording them a good view of the inside. They sparkle an invitation to cross the threshold. That's how The Captain likes his restaurant to be, it's how The Captain insists his restaurant has to be.

Once finished, The Captain steps back a pace for a final inspection. Only when he's satisfied that everything is ship-shape and fully fashioned, Bristol style, does he turn again, back inside.

Now, it's into the bowels of the place for him, the kitchen, the restaurant's engine room. This is where, after another cup of tea, The Captain will hole-up until the lunch trade's finished and the 'closed' sign's hanging from the door.

Already there's the boiling of stockpots and the preparing of sauces to attend to. There's also, for The Captain, a general checking of everything in readiness for this particularly busy day ahead. This is that day of the week when all the lunch-time tables are marked 'reserved' even before the doors are opened. This is the day when The Captain caters for a tour coach, yours, in fact, as advertised all those months ago.

The Captain could do more of this type of business he knows, as some of his competitors do and the coach companies are always urging him to undertake. The Captain, though, shrewd as ever, has decided once a week of this type of work is more than sufficient.

For one thing, the work's intense for all of them with forty-two mouths needing to be fed simultaneously. It's not that The Captain nor his Wife are shy of work but the other consideration, which The Captain takes very seriously is that margins are thin on deals like this especially for the effort required.

Whilst The Captains likes to see his sea chest full, once a week of this type of work is enough, he feels, to help maintain an even keel in the coffers.

Around a similar time, perhaps a shadow later than The Captain, the other restauranteurs and café owners start to follow his sea-boots, as they too begin their preparations for the day. None of them though are quite as prompt and few of them quite as particular as The Captain. This all goes some ways to explain why The Captain's Table is already building a wider reputation and theirs aren't. The Captain intends seeing that that reputation's maintained.

Not all are as particular as The Captain except, perhaps, just one, the Fish and Chip shop, The Saucy Cod, a business whose name alone is sufficient to attract attention without its concomitant logo.

Its owners' scrub and bleach inside and out, on a daily basis, proffering a challenge to any germ desperate to run their hygiene gauntlet. Like The Captain's Table, the Saucy Cod too has built an enviable reputation on the quality of its offering. It's another reputation its owners are anxious to preserve.

∞

Reputations are hard to gain but so easy to lose as the gift shop, Cornish Crafts, which stands on the quay next but one to The Captain's Table can testify. This business, unlike its near neighbour, is very unsure of itself these days.

It's certainly well down from the giddy heights of its former glory, from days when it knew what it was and proclaimed itself as such, hence its name, simple but to the point. In those days it was perfect marketing.

Cornish Crafts was also, in its day, a destination shop. It was the sort of place people would make a special trip to visit.

These days though, under its present ownership, Cornish Craft's become a business that's flaying around in a whirlpool of indecision. It's become locked in a permanent state of flux, its commanders unable to decide on which course it should be heading.

Having purchased the business, which was trading very successfully at the time, the new owners couldn't decide whether to leave it as it was or change it to a shop selling more, well, tourist tripe. Their basic problem is that they've absolutely little to no idea about the venture they've invested in and, so far, have decided to do a mix and match operation which has failed on every front.

Much of their problem, apart from a general inability that is, seems to stem from the fact that they're more absorbed with the intricacies of their personal relationship. They tend to focus on that rather than their business even at this time of the year. It's generally noted and commented on in the village, that their relationship's something which seems to absorbs the bulk of their energies.

They're also a salesman's dream these two and will buy from almost any rep who walks through their door. Under their stewardship, the shop's become a confusion of discordant product, a hotchpotch of incompatibles all vying for ascendency, an unhappy and uncomfortable marriage not dissimilar to that of the owners.

The shop's no longer a centre purely for some of the finest crafts that can be found within the county, as its name continues to suggest, but is now mixed with newer items that are no more than pure junk.

How the shop might wish its old owners to return and take charge again. It would love to have them remove these bronzed and silvered piskies that sit on bits of rock, are attached to key rings, or are made into broaches all of which proclaim good fortune.

These, and other items of tat, usually of foreign origin, compete for the limited space with vases of a delicate beauty; mugs, hand-thrown and bowls, all individual in their design and decoration. The pottery's ashamed to be associated with such bric-a-brac though, for its part, the bric-a-brac's unforgiving of the pottery for its snobbishness.

Generally speaking, nine o'clock's too early a time for the gift shop owners to be in post with the singular exception of Bob Braintree, co-owner with his wife Betty, of the aforementioned Cornish Crafts. At around this time, both in and out of Season, Bob can be seen walking between home and shop with his trusty companion, Blackwood, trotting at his side, more dog-like than the cat that he is.

They offer a strange combination to visiting eyes, these two and have been the subject of many a photograph over the years. What these takers-of-photographs don't know though, is that these two, man and cat, have a strong bond, forged in their common hatred of Betty.

In fairness, Betty dislikes them with an equal intensity, feeling disadvantaged as she does in not having any companion of her own to counter-balance Bob's. It's Betty, though, not Bob, who buys Blackwood's food every day when she does the morning shop. Blackwood tends to forget that when it comes to taking sides.

Blackwood, a slim and wiry black cat of varied parentage and ancestry, had walked into Treddoch Harbour and Bob's life early one frosty morning looking both cold and hungry. Where he'd come from no one knew though, it was assumed, he was a farm cat, semi-wild as he was.

He was a small, slim thing who made up for his lack of size by his attitude, hissing and spitting at everybody that approached as he did. Ironically, it was something that didn't faze Bob; Bob was well used to much the same reception from Betty.

Blackwood is black in colour as his name suggests. The cat might have preferred something a little more original, in his naming, but looking at the shambles that's Cornish Crafts, Blackwood soon realised that Bob's a human of confused thinking and little imagination.

Given his humble origins, Blackwood can only sigh at the fact that Bob hadn't given him a more stylish name though, one that might have elevated his status in the feline world. He would most definitely have preferred a name that had a little more of a ring to it; one that might have been more appealing to the rather regal Bastet. Bastet's made her position quite clear; she's out of bounds as far as Blackwood's concerned.

Blackwood did try muzzling in there in the early days. He'd approached Bastet with a jaunty, nonchalant walk and a casual swish of his white-tipped tail. However, a snarl from Bastet followed immediately with a swift and damaging uppercut from a right paw, edged with razor-sharp claws, quickly convinced Blackwood that Bastet and he were not in the same league.

These days Blackwood's set his aspirations a little lower, having formed a liaison with a tabby, two doors down. Coming from similar backgrounds Blackwood has had to accept that this is a much happier and more sensible relationship altogether.

"Morning Captain."

"Morning Bob, lovely morning. Going to be a hot one," as The Captain, without breaking stroke, continues with his spit and polishing this fine summer's morning.

"Is for now," muses a stationary Bob, but there's a storm brewing. I can feel it. He looks backward, along the path he's walked, as if expecting to catch his first sighting.

To an outsider, it might seem an unusual comment, given it's spoken on such a perfect summer's day but The Captain nods, fully understanding the meaning of Bob's words. He's grateful for some activity so he doesn't have to pursue the conversation further and in order to change the subject altogether turns his attentions to Blackwood, a less contentious issue by far.

The cat's attitude towards humans, apart from Betty, has

softened in the last couple of years; he's now quite happy for The Captain to give him a stroke behind the ear,

Bob and Betty, both short and dumpy in appearance, not unlike a matching cruet set, originate from somewhere in Essex. They've already lived in Treddoch these past five years and will probably continue to do so for some time yet, or until they kill each other, whichever comes the sooner.

The Braintrees have a toxic relationship built on a mutual dislike, a dislike that's only deepened with the passing of years. These days they're two people only happy with the other's misery.

Their association was poisonous almost from the day it began and has only been elevated to its present level of murderousness with the progress of time. Moving to Treddoch hasn't improved things either; if anything, it's served to exacerbate the situation. At least, when they lived in Essex and worked in London, they were out of each other's company for much of the day, weekends excepted, which suited the both of them. Now that they're almost constantly together they bicker, virtually, incessantly.

It's strange that they are a couple, these two; they've loved imperfectly from the very beginning. They'd met at university where they'd read opposing subjects, Bob's a science, Betty's an arts, and they've remained opposed ever since.

Why they'd come together in the first instance is shrouded in mystery even to them, for theirs definitely isn't a match made in heaven. If it was made anywhere it must have been forged under the auspices of the opposition, so hot and venomous is it, each being the poison that laces the other's blood.

The one and only thing they do agree on is that, for the both of them, life seems to have been thirty years of hell. Their mutual dislike for each other though has now grown to such intensity that neither can leave for fear, that in doing so, they may bring the other party a certain degree of peace and happiness they would otherwise wish to deny them.

Bizarre as it seems, their almost near hatred of each other is a kind of love, albeit of a peculiar kind; they're umbilically connected these two. They can never part. For one thing, who else would have them, want them even, if not each other, and they do want each other in their particular way. Where would the one be without the other to hate? They spar off of each other. It's part of their relationship. It is their relationship.

Normally, their dysfunctionality is constrained to the bickering, though on occasion, this level can be elevated to the more lively, even tempestuous you might say. Betty's prone to throwing things, especially when her anger and frustration reach fever pitch, and, by 'things', it's anything in fact. It's usually the first object that comes to hand which can range from the quite small to the very large which Betty really shouldn't be hurling at someone. Given that that 'someone' is Bob though, Betty really doesn't care.

It's fortunate for Bob that Betty's aim's not all that good, especially if he can keep sufficient distance between them. In her time, Betty's taken out two television sets, an antique mirror, a bonus to Bob's mind as he'd always hated it, the mirror having once belonged to Betty's mother, an *art nouveau* jardinière and a lampstand. They were all collateral damage.

The obliteration of one of the television sets still remains Betty's most spectacular achievement to date, not only causing the set to catch fire but throwing out the whole of the house's electrics at the same time. With sparks flying, literally as well as metaphorically, on all fronts, Blackwood had headed for the safety of the garden as fast as four legs could carry him, returning only when hunger and a rain shower overrode fear.

As pleasant and polite as he always is whenever he happens to see them, The Captain can never understand them, these two that fight as demons, try as he might. Theirs is the very antithesis to his own marriage.

The Captain's Wife, as sound as ever, tells him not to even attempt an understanding, just accept what is. The Braintree's relationship is far removed from the steady, reliable one that's hers and The Captain's.

The Trendy Young Couple, as they're still referred to in the village, even after eighteen months of living there, having finished their trendy breakfasts of muesli and decaffeinated coffee would normally be undertaking their domestics before thinking of opening their shop. Not this morning though. Everything has ground to a halt. It's as if they're suspended in time. She's sitting on a chair, a recently delivered letter open on her lap. She's just staring at it.

"Stop worrying," he tells her. "It's not that bad."

"Isn't it?"

"No, and you know it isn't. People are already beginning to forget. Give it a bit longer and they'll have forgotten altogether."

"Are you sure?" she asks, looking worryingly up at him as he puts his arm around her shoulder to comfort her.

"Of course, I'm sure. Just give it till the end of next season. It'll all be forgotten by then and we can go home," he says, with his fingers mentally crossed behind his back as he speaks.

"I hope you're right."

To try and take her mind from it he quickly changes to the

more mundane. "Put it away for now. You've got the ironing to do while I finish the washing-up and take the rubbish out. It'll soon be time to open the shop."

∞

Tom Penhale is out and about for the second time this morning, standing, as he's stood for many a morning during his later life, on the bridge that spans the river. It's the point where the clear waters of the little stream throw themselves shamelessly, almost wantonly, over the last of the stones to tumble into the harbour before rushing out for seas and oceans far distant from the Cornish hills in which they were spawned.

Tom's of that generation when education was rudimentary, leaving school as he did at fourteen to go fishing. University was something he'd heard of but had no connection with. As far as Tom was concerned it wasn't for the likes of him. Education beyond the basic level wasn't something he felt compelled to acquire nor have a need of. Tom knows how to read his bank statements and is fully aware, down to the penny, of just how much money should be in his account which is always more than he has personally ever had need of, having no one to spend it on. Tom lives alone you see.

Now an elder of the community, Tom, who is revered as the oldest fisherman in Treddoch, though he's long hung up his nets and sold his boat, the 'Mary Helen', is, this morning, all Sunday scrubbed, best sweatered and wearing his finest pair of worsted trousers.

Tom's waiting to catch the early bus into the nearby town, a journey of some four miles to the west by road. It's only a little over half of that by water he reflects. For Tom, now in his latter years, a trip to the town has become a big event, venturing little further than the village centre as he does these days.

The local bus, old but still serviceable, will be leaving Treddoch at ten o'clock from the car park. It's a piece of land now that's nothing more exciting than a patch of black tarmac but was once a grass lush meadow bundled with buttercups and lady smock for the cows that so few can remember, to feed upon; certainly, none that are much younger than Tom.

Departure is reasonably prompt, though timing can be slightly adrift especially if Lorraine, the driver, sees a need to finish a conversation with one of her passengers first, or complete a transaction, for Lorraine also has a smallholding on the outskirts of the village. At times, it might seem that the bus doubles as a mobile shop. The owner of both vehicle and service makes no complaints though, Lorraine always ensures he has a regular supply of the freshest of eggs.

Today's offering is somewhat meagre by general standards; eggs, collected and lettuces cut fresh just prior to Lorraine leaving for work. Although meagre, it is, at least, quality assured.

Runner beans and bunches of sweet peas can be expected shortly she reports, whetting the appetites of her seasoned regulars.

Whatever the reason for a delayed departure it's important to remember that, in such a close-knit community, priorities have to be observed and, as the bus will arrive directly, Lorraine sees little issue with the exact time of its departure. Neither do her passengers to whom five minutes here or there is of no great matter, unless they've a train to catch. Given that the train's tabled to leave ten minutes before the bus is scheduled to arrive any local venturing abroad by rail knows not to connect via the bus service anyway.

Casting aside infirmities of age, for Tom no longer strides with the speed of youth, he calculates that it will still take him a good half hour or so to walk from the quay to the bus stop. It's not that the distance is that great, but it's inevitable he'll meet people on the way that he knows. It will be an opportunity for Tom to tell anyone who cares to listen about his impending trip. Such is its importance to Tom in his otherwise now non-eventful life.

Tom's whole life has been interconnected with the village, particularly on and around its foreshore, apart from The War years, when, barely old enough for the task, he'd served, physically unscathed, in the Merchant Navy.

This was more than could be said for his two schoolboy friends, Peter and George who, soldier-like, had together, taken the bus out of Treddoch one Spring morning 'to do their bit' and, together, had never returned.

As the years have drifted and older generations have in their turn passed, memories of those two young hopefuls have faded away until now they're little more than names on a memorial cross to be read aloud every year, honoured, and then put back till the following. Tom might seem to have been more fortunate, but it's all a matter of perspective.

Tom has always had a boat, seemingly since the day he first walked. The sea isn't so much in Tom's blood; it is his blood. Just as some are born with a silver spoon, so Tom was born with an oar.

After the War he returned to fishing for his livelihood, staying inshore though for crab and lobster to be sold on to the local restaurants. To some, Tom's life might be seen as a simple existence but he'd already had his fair share of rolling around mid-ocean, as he would describe it. He was happier when closer to land so he could keep his village in sight.

It also made commercial sense, for that was the time when Treddoch was at the height of its popularity and prosperity, frequented by the 'better off'. Trade was good, money flowed. Lobster was a speciality and Tom knew where to find them.

This former fisherman lives alone in what might now be considered, in Sunday supplement parlance, a 'quaint cottage', adjacent to the quay. It had been his parents before. It's the only house Tom's ever known except for a brief period, after The War, when, married. He'd rented a small place for himself and Mary, nearby.

Though living alone Tom never sees his status as single. He's always regarded himself as being married though that was a long age ago. Technically speaking, Tom's a widower.

Tom had married his childhood sweetheart, Mary, Mary Helen, the 'Mary Helen' immortalised in his boat. They'd been 'courting', as it was in those days, but The War came and Tom went from the harbour of his boyhood straight into the swell of a full-blown Atlantic, ferrying whatever was needed, wherever it was needed.

Shipping from one coast to the other, Tom had escaped the U-boats with probably more luck than he was entitled to. Perhaps it was there that he'd used up all his share of good fortune at one go, he'd sometimes wonder in later life.

Mary had promised to wait and wait she did. They married in a post-war bliss which didn't last long for Mary soon fell pregnant but died during the birth, as did the little girl she'd been carrying.

Tom had to blame somebody so God, in particular, and The Chapel, as His earthly representative to Tom's way of thinking, took the brunt of his rage. After that, when all of his railing and ranting had finally ebbed, Tom ran silent, never discussing the subject again, nor attending Chapel in any shape or form either, despite the attempts of all and sundry to change his mind.

Tom even refused to have Mary's body taken there before she was buried, much to the mortification of The Minister, electing instead, for a simple graveside ceremony, the same as he's about to organise for himself. Hence Tom's visit to town today, to his solicitor, to write his will.

There was an elderly woman at the time, someone who, in those days, might have been called a crone for her witch-like appearance both in her style of dress and her pointed features. She also walked with a stoop and used a stick for support. She always wore full-length skirts and heavy leather boots that seemed well matched. Her eyes were as black as she dressed. She held a reputation for a viperous tongue.

The Old Woman was insensitive to Tom's or anyone's situation for that matter, being a woman used to saying it as it came, unfiltered, in an unconscious torrent. She was also someone unused to having her words challenged. She told Tom that if he didn't hold a proper service (by which she meant, 'in Chapel') for Mary then he would surely burn in Hell.

A young and grieving Tom, usually so quiet and polite, but now someone weighed down with the burden of loss and whose vocabulary had only recently been enriched by a stint of time served as a Merchantman, glaringly retorted, "Bollocks." It was delivered with such a vehemence that it shook and reeled the Old Woman and those about.

Abashed and speechless, she couldn't even think of a reply, before Tom had turned and walked. He never returned to the fold again, not from that day to this. Bystanders, for the most part, silently applauded, some secretly wishing it might have been them who had had the courage to say what Tom had said.

There were those in Treddoch, at the time, who said The

Old Woman had a heart as black as her clothing and subsequently and genuinely, thought her a witch. Many would cross the road, to walk on the other side when they saw her approach, so terrified were they of what they felt even a close proximity to her might bring to them. Others, probably of a more sensible disposition, just viewed her as an unpleasant old woman which is, most likely, exactly what she was.

Few could remember what she'd been like in her younger days, but certainly, the loss of her only son, young, to the sea, his body never to be recovered couldn't have been anything to aid her temperament or character.

The Old Woman had turned to God in her time of loss, in contrast with Tom who turned his back because of his.

The Vicar at the time, in the interests of interdenominational harmony, had kept both his counsel and his distance in the matter. It was, after all, a Chapel affair. His own problems were sufficient for the day.

Tom had never married again though there had been offers which he'd always politely declined. Generally, he just fished and slept, fished and slept with basic domestics in between as necessary. The sea, he found, helped absorb much of his sorrow.

The only exception to Tom's general pattern of life has been Sunday, though not for religious reasons anymore. It's simply that every Sunday, without fail, without regard to season, Tom has visited Mary's grave to give her fresh flowers just as he'd done each week of their short, married life. Mary's birthday, their wedding anniversary and Christmas occasion bonus visits. A girl should always have flowers, Tom has thought.

Though short-lived, Mary has always been long loved.

It's only very recently that Tom's realised he hasn't written a will, has barely ever even thought about it. Not that he's a lot to bequeath, he feels, just a sixteenth-century cottage in a much sought-after location and a little over a hundred thousand pounds in the bank.

To some, it might all seem a small fortune, but to Tom, without Mary, the cottage is just somewhere to eat and sleep, keep the rain off his head, the cold out of his bones. The stone and slate themselves hold no value to him. As for the money in the bank, it's surplus to his needs; an excess from his labour for which he's little personal use or requirement.

As long as Tom had his boat that was all that was required. He's never needed a car so has never learned to drive. He's never been on holiday. He's seen as much of the world as he's ever wanted to see during the War he's always said. After that, he's been content to stay close to his harbour, as content as he can be without his Mary.

As we visit Treddoch today, not only is age catching up with Tom as he accepts it must, more significantly, he feels it catching up with a quickening gait. There's nothing specific that he can quite point to, certainly not medically speaking, but age and its co-conspirator, weariness has crept, surreptitiously, from somewhere behind and have seized his shoulders, sudden, fierce and with an iron grip, a grip that's tightening ever faster.

He's been feeling their proximity for some while now but this morning, warm and bright as it might be, Tom's feeling the cool of their shadows hanging over him. He's sensing their presence and their demands even more strongly; hence his observation when he encountered The Captain, earlier.

They're not only weighing on Tom but, this morning, they seem to be weighing more heavily than ever. He even looks up, half in the expectation of seeing something physical, hanging above him. There's nothing, of course, but, all the same, Tom knows they're there, waiting and, somewhat to his own surprise, he finds he has neither the will nor the wish to combat them. Tom knows only too well that everything must pass, himself included.

Increasingly aware of his own mortality, Tom's begun to sense an ending. Not that it's bothering him in any way; in fact, it's somewhat the opposite. He seems to be in full acceptance. He's now almost welcoming it.

Life for Tom's been long and tedious without his Mary and he's beginning to see her more and more frequently as he settles for the evening, her hand outstretched towards him, silently calling. He knows that his days are growing shorter, and quickly too. He's decided that it's best he gets his affairs in order whilst he still can.

Tom has nephews and nieces, great ones too, all of varying ages and appetites. They're all very nice in their way but none particularly special. There's none he feels a need to leave a bequest to, none, that is, except one, a great-niece who has always visited Uncle Tom ever since she was a little girl and visits almost daily still, even though she's now grown. The odd exceptions are usually due to Little People issues.

Lizzy is the great-niece in question. Tom knows she doesn't have much in life, materially speaking, but she does have a big heart and that counts a lot to Tom. She checks in on him most days, fetching bits of shopping for him if she feels he's neglecting himself and doing some general chores that she senses a man, especially of Uncle Tom's age, might readily choose to ignore.

Although he's never said it, and wouldn't, Tom likes the attention. He looks forward to Lizzy's visits, much as he might scold her for wasting her time on an old man.

"You need to find yourself a younger one than me," he often

admonishes her. It's all bluster of course for in Lizzy Tom sees an incarnation of a daughter that only ever might have been.

Tom particularly enjoys it when Lizzy brings the Little People with her and always finds a few coins in the recesses of a trouser pocket for sweets.

"Uncle Tom, you shouldn't. You can't afford it and it only spoils them." Lizzy, like most of Treddoch's inhabitants, has no concept of the depths of Tom's pockets.

The Little People, like little people everywhere in a similar situation, fervently hope Uncle Tom will ignore their mother. With heads bent back and faces smiling, they look to Tom and say, "Thanks, Uncle Tom," clutching their coins in tight little fists. For them, t's treasure not to be lost; for Tom, it's treasure gained. He finds it wonderful to have someone to spoil, if only for a borrowed moment.

It had suddenly occurred to Tom, one evening, only a week or so before, standing jadedly there on the harbourside, gazing into the lazy waters as they swished and swashed against the boats at anchor, that there was something he could do for Lizzy in return for all her kindnesses of the years. What little he felt he did have he would leave to her. It would be a home for her and the Little People and there was a bit of cash to modernise the place as he knew it needed. Tom isn't completely insensible to his surroundings, just indifferent.

The money in the bank has accumulated over the years. Tom's spent very little on himself and even less on the house. No doubt Mary would have spent more, had she lived, but she hadn't and so Tom didn't.

Standing on the harbourside this summer morning, seagulls circling overhead in a blue clear sky, Tom thinks of Mary, as he so often does, and, also today, of Peter and George, whom in general now, he so often doesn't.

Over the years the friends of his youth have dimmed to little more than faded faces in a crumpled school photograph, a snapshot of frozen time, which Tom keeps in a drawer of his dresser, along with other assorted oddments such as string and pens. By contrast, the picture of Mary stays fresh and alive, for Tom keeps that in a quiet corner of his heart.

∞

Eventually, even Johnny has to stir his board-stiff and lethargic body, albeit at a somewhat steadier pace than much of the rest of Treddoch Harbour, this sun-bright morning. The warm light has caused many of them to leap from their beds with unexpected springs in their steps, a lightness in their hearts and joyfulness in their greetings. The best that Johnny can muster, in comparison, is to let one leg drop to the floor whilst keeping the rest of his body prone. If Johnny does have a spring it's currently rusted fast.

Johnny also has little perception of time and space, other than that the sun is by now further warming his febrile form. He needs to take something for the pains but that means heading, from wherever he's currently resting, towards home. This, in turn, means running the gauntlet he's sure he'll encounter, for he'll have to walk through the village to their one bedroomed flat on the far side. He can already imagine some of the looks he'll get, particularly from a portion of the older women who'll just stare at him as he passes but say nothing. Their scowls can be even more cutting than their tongues.

Groping for strands of reality and struggling to understand where he's positioned in both the physical and temporal senses, Johnny searches, detective-like, for any clue that lurks within the murky sub-terrain that's currently posturing as a mind. Anything, no matter how minute will do. Any memory that can shed light, though, perhaps not quite as harsh as the morning's sun which is already straining his ill seasoned eyes and compounding the drubbings inside his skull.

Alcohol. He remembers that. Lots of it. Too much by all accounts. The Schooner Inn. That too is sailing into view. A merry evening; a heavy night. Very heavy. Why he's finished up where he now finds himself is still a mystery though. He can't, as yet, understand why he didn't return home.

O yes! Abi. Now he remembers why. Clearly, it seemed a good idea at the time, under the guidance of alcoholic thinking. In the harsh reality of morning, he's not quite so sure. He doubts he'll find her mood improved, suspecting, in fact, quite the opposite, given his failure to return last evening and the warnings he's had.

A cat; he also remembers a cat. For some reason a cat looms large in his memory bank. And eyes. Yes, eyes. Definitely eyes. But unnatural eyes. Big eyes. Black eyes. Unearthly eyes. Eyes of a Satanic black that would suck him in if he dared stare too long, he feels and shudders at the thought. It was the eyes.

As much as they might send a shiver through his body the memory of those eyes also grips him. Johnny tries to shake their recollection but loses the battle. They were too mesmeric coming as they did from a feline Svengali.

As memories return, albeit in random order, Johnny remembers that the cat was, in fact, The Cat, Bastet. He'd never noticed her eyes before, but then, he'd never taken that much notice of The Cat before, not in detail. Equally, of course, he'd never ben up that close and personal to the cat as he had been earlier on. He remembers again her fishy breath which only serves to make him retch.

Now he's noticed the eyes Johnny feels compelled to remember. Bastet is long gone but has clearly left her mark on him, in more ways than one, he thinks, as he rubs his hand over his chest where her claws had trod earlier. "Bloody cat!" he mutters and groans as he does so. Even the simplest of speaking hurts.

Rising sluggishly, the second foot gingerly meeting with the ground, Johnny holds his bending head with unsteady hands, frightened almost least it should fall off and roll away. That's how it feels at this moment.

"Never again," he groans. "Never again." But how many times has he said that only to renege once the beer starts flowing and he holds centre stage.

"I can't, I won't, I shan't," he tries to insist to himself, but knows, instinctively, in his weakness, that he probably will. Equally, with neither life nor love heading in a good direction even Johnny, addled as he is, can see that he needs to amend his ways, and fast. He needs a jolt and a big one at that; one of thunderbolt proportions.

Those were Bastet's thoughts exactly when she went hunting for Johnny earlier this morning.

Abi, dispirited, dejected, disconsolate Abi, tired and worn from endless rounds of work and conflict with Johnny, rises, as empty of heart as she's empty of bed. Sliding from under the duvet she puts her feet into her fluffy slippers.

"Fluffy slippers," she thinks. "Good grief! Where's the romance gone, Johnny? We did use to have romance, didn't we? Once. Fluffy slippers," and she shakes her head.

From an empty bed Abi wanders into an equally empty living room then showers, dresses, and breakfasts, though with little appetite for either the food or the day in front of her. Those early moments should have been her sweetest, snuggled next to Johnny, but weren't; they were her coldest, even on this warmest of midsummer's morning.

It's quite clear that Johnny's not even made a guest appearance this time. Normally, after such an evening, he's usually to be found slumped in his chair in the lounge where Abi can at least have the satisfaction of giving his legs a sound kicking just to annoy him. It has little effect on Johnny, he fully accepts it as part of his anticipated punishment, but, if nothing else it does at least help Abi relieve some of her pent-up tensions. It's better than screaming, she thinks and letting the neighbours know of their situation, as if they don't already.

It's nearly time for work, but on an unknown impulse, Abi reaches into the back of the wardrobe where she's preserved the portraits Johnny had so wondrously painted of her all those dreams ago.

Abi really doesn't know why she's taken them out other than, perhaps, as part of some sort of final gesture; she's not looked at them since, since she can't remember when. They're so much more part of a past rather than a present and at this moment hardly indicative of a future, of any sort.

Sitting there, on the edge of the bed, Abi gently runs her fingers over them, these pictures of a time past. There's almost the ghost of a smile on her lips from the fond remembering of happier times when life was light, and a warm-white future seemed the more probable rather than the cold-white of current reality.

"Where have you gone, Johnny?" she wonders, in more ways than one.

Is that really her with such a flirtatious ponytail, pink lips and perky breasts or is it just a memory of someone she once knew? Someone seen in a dream. Fact and fiction blur so readily these days. Abi's tiredness blinds them as they blind her.

Glancing at the bedside clock, Abi makes a hasty exit for work, the paintings left recumbent on Johnny's unslept side of the bed. She'll tidy them away when she returns.

Closing the front door behind her Abi's thoughts on Johnny are an equal mix of love and despair. "O Johnny," she silently thinks, choking back a sob.

Within only minutes of Abi's leaving, Johnny makes it home pretty much unscathed which is surprising, given that his slow pace of walk should have marked him out as an easy target. For all his foreboding though, there were few ill-wishers about this morning and Abi, as we already know, has left for work.

Johnny's particularly lucky not to have bumped into Duncan Thomas, his arch-rival. At least that's how Duncan perceives their relationship. Johnny has no comprehension of such. He's the least critical person of Duncan's work, certainly much less critical than Duncan is himself. Duncan's fully aware of his limitations. It's been eating into him for years, especially after Johnny's star rose over the horizon.

Duncan is a fellow artist, though one of a severely lower grade to Johnny. Whereas Johnny's boats cut through the waters, parting the waves as they go, leaving wash and seagulls in their wake, Duncan's are stubby little tubs, more akin to corks than boats. They seem to do little more than bob on the spot.

His interpretation of people is equally as lifeless as Johnny's is lifelike.

Duncan had wandered into Treddoch one day, much as many another stray before him when he was in his mid-fifties. He'd taken early retirement from the bank in Slough where he'd worked, lived and breathed for thirty-five years. He'd always wanted to paint, to be an artist and had spent a good proportion of his spare time in practice, although, with little success. He'd been much better at counting coppers.

Duncan had believed that the problem lay more with the lack of time and opportunity that he'd so far had, to be able to fully immerse himself in his work, rather than his own, general, lack of ability.

Accordingly, after retirement Duncan had upped sticks and headed for the south-west, settling on Treddoch Harbour as much for the sake of prudence as the quality of the light.

Although in benefit of a company pension Duncan had felt that a belt and braces job was necessary to ensure a comfortable future and looked for a suitable business to invest in. The Village Gallery, in Treddoch, happened to be on the market at the time and showed a healthy set of accounts. It satisfied all Duncan's requirements.

Duncan bought and settled into a new life. He went so far, even, as to buy a smock, a short, red-spotted scarf and a beret which he sported at a jaunty angle. Now, every inch an artist and with his own gallery, there could be no more excuses. Duncan had both time and opportunity to immerse himself in his craft, but his work never really improved, for all his efforts.

The problem for Duncan was, and still remains, he's a man of figures, a man of exactitudes. His mind never could flow freely, certainly nowhere as freely as Johnny's although Johnny's mind, at times runs, perhaps, just a touch too free. Johnny might benefit, even a little, from some of Duncan's exactitude; certainly, as far as life itself is concerned, if not his art.

Duncan's fingers, for all his trying, remain stiff and inert. They hold his paintbrush in much the same manner as they hold his broom each morning as he sweeps his step.

If there's ever been any connection between Duncan's thought process and his hand it leaks out somewhere along the way, probably around the elbow for none of Duncan's creative imaginings ever quite reach the canvas; not properly.

Duncan has become annoyed, almost to the point of being apoplectic, at the raw deal he believes Fate has dealt him. Why wasn't he given the talent that Johnny enjoys, he often wonders. He'd make proper use of it, not squander it as Johnny seems to.

The situation's only exacerbated by the fact that Johnny's always so polite about Duncan's work. He's never said anything derogatory, which makes him possibly the only person that hasn't.

On entering the flat Johnny heads pointedly for the kitchen. A cup of tea, builders' strength, and some medication for his head are priority. From there he lumbers into the lounge where he slumps into a chair to sleep off the final effects of the previous night's revelries.

# Ten O'Clockish

As the clock swings past nine-thirty, the remnant of shop keepers miraculously begin to appear on stage, some, it must be said, with more alacrity in their steps than others.

The newer owners are, inevitably, still enthralled and entranced with the novelty of it all, whilst the more seasoned ones are pretty sure what the day will bring and how it will play out. For them, all of the surprises have long gone with the repetition of days.

So, with varying degrees of activity and enthusiasm and much like The Captain earlier, they begin to wash and wipe at finger-marked windows and tainted paintwork. They sweep away yesterday's debris from their doorsteps, dust and vacuum interiors and adjust stock to slightly more appealing angles whilst checking that price tickets are correctly in place. Once done, they'll man their tills, all ready for today's impending trade and, with the weather fair and the forecast good, hopes are already running high.

All of this is just about in time for the first of the visitors who, lemming-like, are making their way from the car park and heading towards the sea, though not with the same rush. Meandering from shop to shop they pause as necessary, happy to browse the wares on offer as they pass. For once they've plenty of time in otherwise demanding lives.

∞

Amongst this motley assortment of shopkeepers is Patience, a tall, straight-backed, elegant lady, of maturing years, who exudes a certain air of grandeur as she walks.

Having already briefed herself on what's happening in the outside world, Patience is now ready to get fully abreast of events in her more local area. She dislikes the winter when her shop's closed. She's so much less reason to be out and about. So much less chance of finding someone for a bite of conversation and a brief companionship.

Patience is a woman well suited to her name, content as she is to stand and pass the time with all and sundry as she moves between home and shop and vice versa each morning and evening. Patience has never been known to be in a hurry; she's happy to have a conversation with almost anyone.

These days, Patience lives alone, except for her constant companion, the One-Eyed Dog whom she acquired more out of pity than need; no one else seemed to want him because of his affliction. Patience has a kind heart and rarely speaks ill of anyone. She's something of a middle-class version of Lizzy's mother in her light wool twinsets and pearls.

There was a husband, Charles, but he was much older, a gentleman whom no one in Treddoch can really remember. They barely had chance to get to ever to know him, for Charles had died shortly after retiring to the village.

Treddoch was the place Charles had yearned to retire to through all those long years of endless commutes in and out of London. Just as his dream seemed to come to a final fruition, though, so fickle Fortune, in all her perversity, snatched it from him. His goods and chattels were barely out of their packing cases before he was consigned to his.

Patience had slept in a chair downstairs for several nights after Charles had died. She couldn't face their double bed alone, but, one evening, exhaustion beat her and without her even realising what was happening, her feet, on autopilot, led her upstairs. She sobbed bitterly on waking, realising where she was, remembering how alone she was, but, if nothing else, it had broken the spell that bound her. Normal service, or some semblance of it, had to be resumed.

Patience, having no close family anywhere in the country, and no other place in which she particularly wanted to live, decided she might as well stay where she was. She was starting to make a few friends; the village was becoming something of home.

Looking for something to occupy her days Patience opened the small jewellery shop you'll notice on the corner as you walk towards the quay. It's mainly for the companionship, with Charles gone, rather than for the money. Patience is fortunate that her late husband has left her financially comfortable. She doesn't have to worry on that front.

Patience retails, she will tell you, fashion jewellery and other accessories for the more discerning customer. The pieces are all of the sort that she, herself, would wear. They're quite exquisite, in their way, as are her prices. Consequently, she's never overwhelmed with browsers coming into her shop, which suits Patience very well. She wouldn't want to have to deal with masses. There are just enough in number, to her mind, to keep Patience sufficiently occupied and for her to give them all that personal level of service which she always expects herself when shopping.

The One-Eyed Dog accompanies her wherever she goes, standing contentedly whenever Patience pauses for conversation. He's no trouble to anyone, not even himself.

Patience did try leaving him at home, originally but he'd howled incessantly, much to the annoyance of her neighbours. Now, she brings him to the shop each day, where he lies, in his basket under the counter, as quiet as the mouse that's currently inhabiting Patience's loft space. The dog's quieter in fact, for the mouse must wear boots, Patience sometimes thinks, given the noise it makes as it scampers through her loft in the otherwise quiet of the night. She knows she should 'do something' about it. She really should get someone in, but she hasn't the heart.

"It can't be doing any damage, can it?" Patience asks herself.

In answer, Patience just assumes not, though she's never checked. She lives in the unjustified hope that it'll just get bored one day and disappear, much in the same way as the day that it had first appeared. It's not a very rational thought but a kind one as befits Patience's nature.

A few doors from Patience and a little closer to the centre of the village, is another jewellery shop, owned and run by The Trendy Young Couple. It has its own unique and idiosyncratic fashion style, which caused some chatter and shaking of heads amongst the older, more conservative villagers when The Couple moved in. Hence the naming they acquired and have been left to live with.

They moved into Treddoch from Brighton at the beginning of last year and rent the flat above as well as the shop below, which is particularly convenient when a cup of coffee's required, or a sandwich needed, come lunchtime.

Why they've moved to this quiet backwater from the apparent bustle of The Lanes though no one can really understand, and The Trendy Young Couple have never been inclined to offer an explanation. It's nobody else's business is their thought, though there are always those in Treddoch who'd like to make it so.

Not knowing the true reason, theories abound, of course; this wouldn't be Treddoch Harbour if they didn't. These theories range in their breadth from the reasonably sensible to the definitely absurd, but such is the nature of the village, especially when The Season's in full swing. At this time, in particular, a general tiredness takes over and sane thinking gets pushed, not simply into the back seat but way beyond even the boot.

The only common denominator in all the theorising, based primarily on the couple's dress code and the irrational fact that that they've moved from Brighton, is the suspicion of drug involvement, not that anything's ever been remotely proven. It's simply that The Trendy Young Couple look like the sort of people who would probably 'do drugs' to people who don't and aren't the slightest bit trendy themselves. It's more than sufficient evidence in some minds.

Although selling jewellery might seem competitive, theirs is a completely different operation to Patience's. Their shop, bright and gaudy as befits their nature, is in stark contrast to Patience's delightfully demure. Theirs is stock of the tarnishable variety, designed specifically not to last. It's bright and brassy, cheerful and pennies cheap; something to brighten a girl's day for no more than the cost of a latté.

If they are competition, then Patience certainly doesn't view it that way. She's more than happy to be pleasant and polite. It's always a, "Good Morning," as she passes on her way to her own shop and then "I hope you've had a good day" as she passes on her return, towards her cottage and the gin and tonic that's waiting.

The One-Eyed Dog just stands without fuss, tethered to his lead whilst they talk. Patience could disconnect him; he wouldn't run. He's too desperate and too grateful for the company. He remembers life before Patience when no one wanted him.

Some of the shopkeepers are more open about their businesses than others. They will readily say whether it's been a good trading day or not. Patience is the exception. Whenever she's asked, Patience has always had a 'good day' herself but then she couldn't be expected to have experienced anything less than perfect. It's not Patience's way.

This is actually the second trading Season for the Trendy Young Couple. General opinion's already that they won't be staying much longer; one more Season maybe. Like so many who move to Treddoch, it's expected that these too, will leave after their third year. It's abundantly clear that Treddoch's not the place for them; fish out of water and all that. They're clearly used to a life with more of a bustle about it. Just look at the way they dress!

It does seem as if 'general opinion' will come true in their case. Come the end of their second season, when business slows to still and they find little to fill what they feel should be busier lives, they'll start to ask each other, once again, why they came to this quiet backwater in the first place. Why did they desert the bustle of Brighton which they both so much prefer?

They both know the answer, of course, even if it's never discussed. Not openly; not even between themselves. A look between them is sufficient. Like Joan, they too have a past they want to put behind them.

"Give it another year and we'll be able to go back," he says. "Just the one more year."

"I hope so," she replies, somewhat wistfully. "But when I think back," and she shakes her head at her memories.

"Have faith; it'll be alright. You'll see," trying to console her.

"I hope so. Going back, it's all I dream about."

"Just give it one more year. People will have forgotten by then. You'll see."

"I hope you're right."

"I am," and he only hopes that he is for he has the same dream too.


∞


Almost in the middle of the village is a clothing shop, 'Top to Toe', a relatively large shop by village standards and one which caters for both locals and visitors alike. It sells fashionable skirts and tops, dresses, shorts and t-shirts for both sexes, swimwear, and, come either end of The Season, jumpers, as well as a range of footwear to prove the validity of the business name.

The stock's piled high and sold relatively cheaply. It boasts new styles brought in fresh, each week from the rag trade 'up country' much the same as will be selling all over on this bright summer's day. It's an up-to-the-minute fashion house for up-to-the-minute people.

No one in Treddoch now caters for the remnants of that former generation who might still want to buy their long-johns and Guernsey sweaters, their thick stockings and heavy skirts. That was the sort of haberdashery that Old Man Cornish once kept in a shop only half the size. His was the sort of emporium where, in addition to the above, you could buy your needles and pins, your buttons and bows, your threads, your ribbons, your skeins of wool, fabric from the roll and, not to mention your once, all-important, elastic by the yard.

The haberdasher is another trade no longer viable in this changing world of the cheap and cheerful, this world of the disposable, of the immediate. It's another trade whose only remains are to be found in the Treddoch Harbour museum, down on the quay.

The museum, at least's, proving to be a growing business.

Somewhere towards the middle of the village is Duncan's art gallery, Village Art, as it's called though it's a little exuberant to ever really describe it as a gallery. Such a term is far too optimistic, given what the establishment really is.

Village Art is, in fact, little more than a picture shop. It's, quite literally, a shop selling pictures as another might sell sweets or toilet rolls. It's not as if the paintings are of very good quality, let alone have any artistic merit to them. They are of the rather large and gaudy sort, churned out by factories in the far east. They seem to sell, however and have certainly helped provide the shop's owner with a living of sorts over the years. He also has his bank pension.

Duncan Thomas, the wannabe artist, now in his later sixties, is still single. As far as the matrimonial front is concerned, any forays he may have made in that market seem to have been as equally poorly executed as his artistic ones.

Some of the villagers have questioned his sexuality over the years, never having seen him with a woman, though it's fair to say that Duncan's not of any particular persuasion in this regard. Duncan just lives for his art. Sadly, for Duncan, his art doesn't reciprocate the same feelings.

On the plus side for Duncan his painting capabilities, though limited, are just about sufficient for him to be able to leave his easel set up in the shop complete with a part-finished painting. It's something of a focal point when talking with customers; Duncan proudly refers to the item as, 'work in progress'.

Coupled with the paint palette and brushes lying alongside they all help give the place that air of authenticity to those little versed in the subject. These, together with the cravat and paint-smeared smock Duncan permanently wears, all add to the general ambience of the room and act as useful adjuncts to the sales process.

Duncan has become increasingly embittered in his latter years, more so as Johnny's star has come on the rise. Try as he might Duncan just doesn't have Johnny's natural talent, no matter how he sometimes might wish that he did. What he would do with it; the heights he could ascend he often thinks. He wouldn't be stuck in Treddoch, that's for sure, and certainly not selling this rubbish, as he admits it to be, if only to himself. He would have a proper gallery in Newlyn or St. Ives even; an exhibition in London perhaps.

As Duncan knows, or at least believes he knows, these are the places where real art lovers and, better still, collectors gather; people who know art when they see it and are prepared to pay handsomely for it. He certainly wouldn't squander the talent as he sees Johnny doing; he'd make much better use of it. It may be, of course, because Johnny's an artist of exceptional, albeit wasted talent, that he's the character he is, and Duncan can only ever dream of being.

Slightly off the main tourist track, on an almost backwater of the village is a shell shop. I say 'shop', but if you visit, you'll notice that it's actually the front room, now converted, of the home of John and Anne Tregear.

When health issues forced John to sell his fishing boat, sooner than ever envisaged, and stay ashore, he mooched about the house for a week or so before Anne told him in no uncertain terms that he'd better find something to do. Her terms, in fact, were very certain. She didn't want him under her feet all day. Not that he was, he still hung out around the harbour with Tom and the other fishermen but wasn't really achieving anything, just treading time.

Anne saw that John needed a purpose. He was too young still just to be sitting around, telling tales of times past, waiting for the inevitable. As far as Anne was concerned John still had a present and he'd better start living in it. If he didn't then he'd better have a really good, cast iron, bomb-proof reason as to why not; one that would pass muster when he ran it by Anne. John knew he didn't have one, would never find one, definitely not one of the calibre required to be successful against Anne. Such a reason didn't exist.

John's problem was that he'd no idea what else to do apart from fishing. He'd had no hobbies as such. His life very much centred on his work and his family, Anne and the two girls. He did have a small collection of seashells though, mostly ones he'd gathered over the years, together with a few he'd bought. He was fond of his shells. Anne had found him a drawer to keep them in and a few of the better specimens were even allowed out on display.

It was Anne's idea that he opened a shell shop, from their front room. They didn't need the space now, the girls were grown and married. There'd be no rent to pay and if it wasn't successful, why they'd have their old front room back.

It all seemed very simple, but where to source the stock from. Once again it was Anne to take the initiative, suggesting that John visit the owner of the shell shop in the nearby town, a tourist place itself, and ask him. John knew the boy after all. He's the son of an old fisherman friend and there'd be no question of competition, given the miles between them. Anne felt sure the lad would help and he did.

So, two years ago now, John opened for business and in that

time has become something of a shell expert in his way, reading voraciously on the subject as he has. Anne might look at him sometimes and smile quietly, satisfied with what she's achieved for him. She's glad to see him with a purpose again.

On the whole John's well pleased himself although there are the odd occasions, like this morning, when he misses the old harbour and the waters he used to fish. As every morning John takes a walk the few yards to the Quay to chat with Tom among others. He does envy them this day though, their being able to stay out in the summer's sun whilst come nine-thirty he has to be back home, ready to open the shop.

Every morning of The Season, just as he's about to depart for his early walk, Anne, always, without exception, wherever she is, whatever she's doing says, "Now mind you keep an eye on the time. I want you back, nine-thirty sharp, to get this shop of yours open." She always emphasises the 'yours'.

"Don't be late, I haven't the time to do it for you," which isn't true, of course. Anne could easily find the time if needed but she's determined to keep John on track. It's for his own good, she tells herself in that way that wives have when organising the lives of their husbands of over forty years.

Tom is now, settled comfortably on the bus and lost in a jumble of thoughts. There are thoughts, inevitably of the past and especially of Mary as well as thoughts of the present. He thinks about his trip to town today and his reason for it; he thinks of Lizzy and the Little People. He smiles to himself as he remembers how they've brought light into his otherwise shadowed world. He also feels that a change is coming; he can all but smell it on the wind. His sun, he knows, is setting. He's awaiting it with a quiet resignation.

∞

The last of the traders, without exception, to arrive and open are Joan and her partner Henry, owners of the Fudge Shop. They never arrive until the dot of ten, just as the church clock is striking the hour. If the old clock should fail, the villagers will be able to set their timepieces by these two.

The Fudge Shop's sandwiched between the Butchers and Jason Henley's. *'The Fudge Shop'*, the board above the window proudly boasts, as if it's the only one in existence, forgetting that the South West's littered with them through every town and village.

It's not as if the produce sold there's local either. 'Made On The Premises' it definitely isn't. It's just the opposite in fact, very much, 'bought in'. It's dieseled across The Tamar from factories way beyond and boxed there, with a sunshine view of Treddoch Harbour in all its gaudy splendour on the front, giving it the authentic, 'local' look, which is as near as it will ever get.

The Fudge Shop business is a semi-retirement affair, which explains why Joan takes its operation rather casually. She'd rather not have it at all if she were honest, which she isn't always. She only works it to keep Henry happy, for the moment. Manipulative would be a more suitable description of Joan than honest. She's patient too. Joan will get what she wants in the end. She always has, always does.

Henry has absolutely no idea about retail trade in general, nor the confectionary trade in particular, leaving the choice of merchandise entirely to Joan's selecting. Henry just settles the monthly accounts.

As may be gathered, neither of these two players are overly enthused with their business activities. Fortunately, they don't have to be; it's not their primary source of income. The shop's there just to add a little extra cash and was a useful property investment. Moreover, it seemed a good idea at the time.

It was all part of their reasoning for abdicating home and making the move to Cornwall where life, it was assumed, would immediately become wonderful, away as it was from old ties, old habits, old memories. It was to be a new life, together, for the two of them, certainly a new life for Joan.

No doubt, the property will be sold on before long when their owners become too bored with being tied to want to bother with the effort any longer. Rather than admit to it all having been a failed idea Henry will, most likely, make some capital gain from the selling and in so doing find a justification for its original purchase.

Joan and Henry, live in one of the newer properties outside of the village, on top of the cliffs. Sea views are very much included, unless it's the Winter, when such views are often obscured by grey seas of mist that swim inland from the Channel and have a tendency to linger for the day, if only to be an annoyance. They're certainly of no benefit, that's for certain, leaving everything they touch damp and cold, miserable to the core, with no hope of sun. This was never mentioned in the estate agency brochure reflects Henry. Joan doesn't seem to mind; the property is aspirational and, in a price-bracket generally reserved only for in-comers, such as themselves.

Joan and Henry tend not to mix with the Locals socially, though they do observe the common civilities in passing. They see little mutual interface, preferring to keep with their own kind, especially for extra-curricular activities such as drinks, dinner parties, a round of golf and the like where they can all talk nonsense and reminisce about lives left behind which now seem to have been so much glossier. Had they been so in the reality, then why would they have left?

Little is known of either their backgrounds, particularly Joan's, not even amongst their circle of friends. Like The Trendy Young Couple Joan too has a history of which only she knows and which even she tries hard to forget. Though rumours abound, as with The Trendy Young Couple, no one knows the absolute truth; in Joan's case, not even Henry.

All that is known, with any reasonable degree of accuracy, is that Henry has an ex-wife and two, maybe three children who, so far have never visited, somewhere 'up country'. There was also a business Henry now no longer owns. It was in printing, or suchlike; a substantial affair sold off to help with the divorce settlement and provide for the dream that he, and his ex-secretary, now partner, had for themselves. Theirs was a dream away from the grit and dust that they perceived city life to be or, at least, as Joan had perceived city life to be.

Divorced and having nowhere else to go Henry merely followed; he was Joan's ticket out. Although he didn't know it he always was.

Joan had once answered an advert Henry had placed for a PA, well, a secretary really, but PA sounded so much better. It was more in keeping with a rapidly expanding business, a recently acquired golf club membership and holidays that were becoming increasingly long-haul.

When Joan answered the call, Henry saw her as everything he could wish for, both as a PA and a woman. Joan saw Henry as the meal ticket she'd been searching for. Fifteen years his junior and fully in her prime Joan was the epitome of efficiency. All secretarial smiled, tailored to perfection, stocking thighed and heeled of foot Joan soon seduced him, mentally at first, then physically and both to a point of exhaustion.

Day by remorseless day Joan wormed her way, first into Henry's mind with her super-efficiency, then his trousers, soon after that, his life and, ultimately, his bank account, the place where she felt most content.

It's not the money itself though; that holds little fascination for Joan. She isn't like Tamsyn. Joan doesn't revere money for its own sake. Money's not her god. To Joan, money is merely a conduit to the trappings that it can provide. It's the trappings that Joan revers.

The wife of past years, who had been there for Henry as he built his business, client, by client, was suddenly sidelined. The children, three to be meticulous on the point, side-lined themselves, aligning themselves with their mother instead. They loath Joan and only ever wish her ill. They're not, perhaps, the nicest of thoughts, but at least, unlike Joan, they're honest.

For her part, Joan really doesn't care either way. They're not her children so, as far as she's concerned, they're not her problem. Joan grew up hard, in the back streets of somewhere she's never mentioned. She learned to look after herself from very early days although those days are shrouded in a fog, thicker than the ones that occasionally blanket the piece of coast where she now lives. Even today, within her new circle, little is known of Joan's early history. Joan likes it that way.

With Henry firmly secured, Joan had felt it time to create a new life, certainly for herself. Henry, suddenly bereft of a past, and having nowhere else to go, dutifully followed, funding their move as he went. He stoically accepts life as he's made it. There's no going back he knows, even if, in some secret recess, he might, sporadically, wish there was.

Looking back over the events that have unfolded, Henry's come to realise that he hadn't exactly wanted to cut the umbilical cord to his marriage. If he carefully recalls, he hadn't actually ever wanted to start a new life at all. A little fun perhaps; something on the side. Bit of a fling. Last tango and all that before his hair went, his belly grew and senility took the helm. He'd been outmaneuvered and fast. It was checkmate almost before Henry had moved a pawn into position.

On too late a reflection, life had been satisfactory as it was, really. It hadn't been all that bad. It had become a little dull, perhaps, but that was mostly due to the norms of married life he suspected. He'd let himself be seduced by the prospect of something more exciting. There rarely is, as Henry has come to realise.

He'd been seduced, let himself be seduced, to a point where he'd definitely lost control of the situation. Fate, in the form of Joan, had taken charge and she'd charged through his life and marriage at full gallop. Almost a bystander, Henry had been carried along, becoming part of the carnage.

∞

Those of you hoping for a glass of something boasting a stronger bite than caffeine can offer, even at this early hour of day, will need to stay their patience just that while longer yet, for Treddoch's two pubs won't be opening for another hour.

For the now, it's time for their morning sparkle; slate floors have to be scrubbed, wood-work has to be polished, brasses have to be gleamed. Bar cloths are sent for washing whilst fresh, beer-free ones come on as substitute. Old, wood windows of yellowing paint, now somewhat delicate through long exposure to the salted air are cast as wide as their aging hinges, long in need of oil, groaning their resistance, will allow. There's the hope of sea fresh breezes replacing the fog and haze of the last night's revelries and all this in readiness for the reprise.

There are only the two pubs in Treddoch, The Fishing Loft and The Schooner Inn, though historical anecdote suggests that there might have been a third at one time. It's all conjecture, there's no concrete evidence to support such a theory. It's been helpful, never-the-less, in building a myth, somewhat akin to that of the piskies.

Myths and legends are the very foundations that local tourism is built on. In Treddoch's case, the myth is that there'd once been, three chapels, three butchers and seemingly, three pubs in the village. If nothing else it's a nice quirk for the tourist guide and one which it shamelessly exploits.

All that can be quoted with any degree of certainty and authority is that there are, as have been, just the two, as fore-mentioned. The Fishing Loft, out on the quay, is an independent house of reasonably recent origin whilst The Schooner Inn, topside of centre, was originally an inn. In its time it was as much for the benefit of travellers as of locals, with its five letting rooms above what was then an alehouse. It's a little bit chicer now.

# Lunchtime

In total antithesis to Winter, Treddoch, in The Season, is really starting to throb come lunchtime. The sheer number of people thronging the streets could almost make the little place get mistaken for the metropolis. Within a few months, how it will all change; there'll be barely a soul out in the cold and wet more than needs be.

For now, though, there's a vibrancy in the air. It's an almost party atmosphere with a liveliness and bustle will that will carry on well into the afternoon as the earlier number of visitors grows exponentially with the addition of a steady stream of new arrivals. The place is beginning to feel wanted, lived in. In short, it has life.

From the perspective of eating though, this period called Lunchtime can be a variable time slot; anywhere from twelve till twoish. Tourists, on the whole, certainly don't feel tied down to any particular timetable. Neither too, do those serving them.

The only ones tied to a regime these days seem to be some of the older men, the traditional men, the men of crafts, the Masons, the Plumbers, the Carpenters and such like. These are the men, who, in line with time-honored practice, having started work prompt at eight, will still stop prompt on the stroke of twelve.

This little group is still drawn towards home, as if pulled by some beacon, for the cooked meal ready waiting on the hob, wife customarily in attendance. For them, The Season is no different to any other time, other than there are now more people to skirt around.

Those, unused to such traditions, or perhaps with wives who have lives of their own, tend to follow a much less rigid, much less stringent routine altogether. Whilst they too will break for lunch at some point, the timing is less rigorous and the food, generally, more *al fresco*. Theirs is more likely to be a sandwich, plastic-wrapped for both hygiene and freshness, brought with them or a pie or pasty from Jason's oven, still piping hot. In the winter that's considered a bonus, especially if they're working out of doors.

For a few, it's a liquid lunch though that's not always to be recommended, especially on a day as hot as today is. There's likely to be some low productivity in those quarters.

Lunchtime, for those in the tourist trade, is nowhere near as organised. This time of the year, in particular, with The Season starting to build, shopkeepers, generally tend to forage as they go, snacking between customers.

It can be a hurried bite from an apple or sandwich, a crunch of a biscuit even. All are acceptable. When they're excessively busy regrettably, not often enough, they'll be sure to tell you, lunch can get missed altogether; a mug of coffee being an unsuitable substitute. Business comes first, opportunity must be seized. Capricious as it is, it may not visit again.

Whatever they can get it will all have to manage them till they can get home for a 'proper' meal, later on, though their pockets will be well lined with the proceeds of a good day's takings. Life can have its compensations.

Cars and coaches, nose to tail, are snaking their way down the hill in solid descent, steadily filling the spaces, from front to back, in the waiting car park. Engines off, they spew their occupants across the tarmac, leaving them first to fumble in their pockets and purses for ticket machine change.

After that, it's time to strap excited toddlers into pushchairs, fix and angle sunshades, attach leads to panting dogs and help infirm relatives into wheelchairs. It's a reasonable distance to the harbour though fortunately, an even walk.

Their final acts are to grab hats and bags, though nobody will be wanting coats today; this is one definite. These can be safely left behind as all begin to assemble under a burning sky without the benefit of even the slightest hint of a breeze. Few are complaining though. After all, this is what they've come all those miles for.

Some will be bringing home-packed lunches, sandwiches, salads and a sundry collection of accompaniments, whilst others will seek out a snack or two as they walk. Jason's shop usually proves to be popular.

A few are even now salivating at the thought of a 'decent' lunch in a café or restaurant, something alien to their normal workaday world of shop-bought tuck and meal deals that put little strain on the eater's taste buds.

They will also be bringing their dreams, these visitors, with their pre-programmed imaginings of sapphire bright seas, barely moving, struggling as they seem, in the heat of the day, to reach the shore; it's the norm.

There are also dreams of rest and relaxation; dreams of peace. To them Treddoch, locked in its time warp, will seem a world apart; a haven of tranquillity after the haste and chase of town and city life, the rush and crush to work of a morning, its repeat home every night.

A few might even take a dream away. The dream of living here; someday.

∞

The cafes and restaurants are starting to fill their tables. It's just a few, to begin with, but numbers grow as lunchtime reaches its peak and stomach's rumble. It's quite predictable, just as is the rising of the sun again tomorrow. It's the nature of The Season, the way it nearly always goes.

The Captain's Wife is standing behind the restaurant's bar, her normal station, fiddling with some glasses and a small vase of flowers that are already where they're supposed to be. It's just something to keep her hands busy as she waits for half-past twelve. Like her daughters, now in their waitress uniforms and standing to one side, she's all ready to greet the influx as soon as it hits them. Smiles are prepared to be fixed.

The Captain's in his kitchen, at battle stations. Everything's organised and in place, waiting for the go-ahead to be given, all as you might have now come to expect from The Captain. Fully set, he stands unflustered.

Today is the one day of the week that The Captain, albeit somewhat reluctantly, accepts a pre-booked touring party, in this case, yours. A sign at the door announces that the restaurant's fully booked this lunch-time and the tables are all marked 'reserved', to reinforce the message. For you that answered the advert all those months ago, today is the highlight of your trip, remember, a guided tour of Treddoch Harbour and lunch in this, The Captain's Table restaurant, alongside the quay. Your dream come true, if only for a couple of hours.

Looking at his watch the Tour Guide is starting to gather his charges around him as they meander through the village, towards the restaurant. He's had to pick up the pace a bit as some are pausing to browse the shops they're passing. With the experience of having run this excursion many times before, he takes charge, somewhat as Molly might.

"We're booked for twelve-thirty so I do need to chivvy you all along," urges the Tour Guide. He knows The Captain's a stickler for time, "It'll be me that'll be in trouble with The Captain if we run late." That usually works; no one wants to get their Tour Guide into trouble.

"Let's leave the gift shops, for now, there'll be plenty of time after lunch for all that and a trip along the coast if you want. The sea's nice and calm today so that's a good opportunity for you, but for now," and he pauses, "Is everybody here?" They nod in response, though none of them have actually taken a headcount. They may be all there; equally they may not.

The Tour Guide accepts their nodding as affirmation. Experience, again, has taught him it's easier that way. "Excellent, excellent. Let's go in then," and the Tour Guide ushers his flock through the doorway into the stone cool of the interior, giving the Captain's Wife a kiss on the cheek in greeting; after all, he's known The Captain and his family since a boy.

The Captain's Wife is a wonderful hostess, The Captain's, a good cook. They'll make sure today's a day you'll always remember and talk of for years not yet thought.

∞

A small, but sustainable queue is forming at the Fish and Chip shop, The Saucy Cod. It'll be much larger next month as numbers continue to build; impending school holidays are already looming into view. For now, though, The Season's still in its infancy and, in consequence, the column queuing through the door's quite tame in comparison with what's to come later. This comparatively small number's easy for the owners to handle; they'll hardly break a sweat.

The owners, Allan and Jenifer MacDonald are satisfied with the way The Season's progressing so far. So far, it's definitely going to pattern. As long as things hold fast, everything should be alright, come the end but they know, nothing can be taken for granted. No one in Treddoch takes anything for granted until October approaches its finish and the coffers can be officially confirmed as having been duly replenished.

Allan MacDonald, Scotsman by birth, Glaswegian by accent, is a long way from Islands and Highlands, even from the border with England, and has been for some considerable time now. Allan's another who's married a village girl, in his case, Jenifer Trescott.

It should be noted, though, the Trescotts originally came by way of Camborne so, although the family's of solid Cornish extraction, they're not always considered 'local' in village terms.

It was Jenifer's grandfather, a merchant of varied interests and properties, who had made the family's money. A self-made man, Kenver Trescott could have eaten with his snout in the trough, given the level of his wealth at the time, although he never actually did, it should be stated, and no one would have commented. Such was his standing. Sadly, for Grandfather Trescott though, his son, William, was not of the same commercial mind. William never added to the pile; he merely lived off it.

Jenifer's grandfather, Kenver Trescott, as is only natural, wanted to give the boy, William, a much better start to life than he believed he had had, so William was afforded the luxury of a private education. He was sent to public school first, then on to

Oxford for a university. Finally, a place was 'found' in a Truro law practice, where William's father gave the partners, Jago, Jago and Jago (a family firm of only two, one of the Jago's having by then been long deceased) substantial business. They owed, and when the favour was called in, they responded appropriately.

William didn't particularly shine at law; it's quite probable that he wouldn't have shone in anything, whatever he'd attempted. He'd even married later in life than all of his contemporaries. On the plus side though, by the time he did marry he found a wife, Isabella, who was on the younger side. She was pale of face, slim of figure and inordinately attractive, almost ethereally so. She was the sort of girl who could shatter a heart with the merest of glances. Men fell before her. William thought her a bit of a coup.

Isabella was a somewhat fanciful name for those parts and for that time; she liked to claim she was of Spanish extraction originally. It was though, by chance, a name well matched to the body for Isabella was a somewhat fanciful girl in herself and, regrettably, for William and the family fortune, as flouncy of nature as she was of dress.

William was really in need of a woman of iron for his counterbalance. Isabella was more of a wisp. She was the sort who'd only exacerbate the situation, hovering, as she did, just that fraction above the planet's surface. Her feet were never fully earthed.

How the two came ever together isn't quite certain. Being somewhat older than Isabella, William was, in many ways, more of a father figure to her than a lover. No one though, ever once suggested that the Trescott family money might have had any influence on her choice in William, whatever might have been their private thoughts.

If Kenver himself thought anything then he kept it to himself.

He was grateful for the boy to be married at last; hopeful, now, for an heir. Everything came with a cost, Kenver had always believed.

It wasn't that long after the wedding, a year or two at most, that William's father tragically died from something no more complicated than slipping on a piece of ice. His head, regrettably, took the brunt of the fall. By this time, William's mother was already deceased. William, a man more adept at spending money than earning it, inherited.

Isabella, long tired of the grey and granite that she felt characterised her life in Camborne, persuaded the easily persuadable William to leave Jago, Jago, and Jago and retire to Treddoch Harbour where he could lead a more gentlemanly lifestyle. The Manor, to one edge of the village, was conveniently up for sale.

They bought the property and moved from Camborne. Within twelve months Jenifer was born. She was their first, last and only child. After Jenifer, Isabella vowed she'd never go through the birthing process again. It was far too painful and unrefined a process for her delicate tastes.

Over time, the grandfather's inheritance dwindled from a pile to a comparative pittance, though one man's pittance can still be viewed as another man's pile. When William died Isabella sold The Manor and bought a more sensible sized home for herself further into the village. It wasn't that she was exactly begging on the streets, but rather more a case that Isabella couldn't bear the solitude; William had always been there to attend to her. Not only was William dead but by this time Jenifer was grown, married and living in Glasgow, a million miles away by Isabella's estimation.

Allan Barclay MacDonald was born, raised and lived in Glasgow all his life until he moved to Treddoch. Two more contrasting domiciles would be hard to find. Allan has fitted into both as easily as his hands into his fleece-lined gloves and as comfortably. He never compares the two places. An easy-going man, Allan's happy to be in either, as long as he's with Jenifer and can get his glass of Scotch of an evening. It's Allan's one weakness, and one he's not ashamed to admit to either.

Allan first met Jenifer when they were both on holiday, in Spain. He was with a robust group of likeminded young men, Jenifer was with some girls from university. For them finals were over, they were having a break before life, with all the realities therein contained, took over. Jenifer didn't realise that they already had.

Jenifer and Allan established an immediate friendship, which led to romance, to a relationship to marriage and, eventually to Young Kenver, named after a grandfather Jenifer had never known. Kenver MacDonald is part Scot, part Cornish, though combined he's all Celt. As such he's heir to two tartans, neither of which he's sported so far.

Allan worked in the family business in Glasgow, a 'chippy'. It belonged to his parents, as to his grandparents before. Allan, who had started work there straight from school, was well versed in the art of cooking exemplary food at this particular level. His beer batter was already legendary. Jenifer found employment in a local solicitor's office where she fared much better than her father had previously.

Jenifer was now living in a two-bedroomed flat in Glasgow. Born and having lived most of her life at The Manor she would sometimes be asked if she missed it. It was, quite a change after all.

"Not really," she'd reply. It was a big house, true and boasted a lot of space, unlike her flat. On the negative side it was also somehow cold and empty, particularly of love. Love was a comparatively new sensation for Jenifer, something she'd found with Allan. The flat, like The Manor, was irrelevant. To Jenifer, they were just containers for lives.

Isabella, never complaining outwardly, didn't like the distance that separated her daughter from her, and now her grandson. Whenever they visited, she always mourned their return to Glasgow, plotting silently as to how she might retain them. She was getting inexorably older and worried increasingly as to who was going to take care of her. Life, for Isabella, had always been very much about Isabella. Age didn't change anything.

So, Isabella plotted, though to little avail until, one day, unexpectedly, The Saucy Cod, fish and chip shop in Treddoch, was put up for sale. Isabella immediately spotted an opportunity, offering Allan and Jenifer the money to buy the business outright. There was, after all, still a little coin left. There'd be no mortgage, no encumbrance; the business would be their very own.

They couldn't refuse and didn't. They didn't hesitate for a moment. Jenifer returned to Treddoch complete with husband, son and a hamster, named Colin.

> Jenifer had tried to suggest something other than Colin, such as Hamish, or Macbeth even as a name for the hamster. It was, she thought, more appropriate for a hamster that was Scots-born but Kenver would have none of it. A child of developing years can have very set opinions on occasion. So, Colin it was, though, given the short span of life a hamster can expect, no longer is.
>
> Young Kenver and Colin were very close for a time; even as a man, Kenver still remembers Colin with fondness, much as he does his grandmother.
>
> It can only be assumed that Colin was as happy with the move to Treddoch as the three of them, Allan, Jenifer, and Kenver were, given that his most immediate surroundings

had remained totally unchanged. He'd travelled south in his cage in the air-conditioned comfort of the family saloon.

Allan, under very clear and specific instruction from Jenifer, drove particularly carefully, especially on Cornish bends, which only served to lengthen the journey time. After several hundred miles of travel, a tiring Allan could only hope that Colin was appreciative of the efforts made on his behalf.

If those four were happy with the move, then Isabella was ecstatic; she'd had her own way at last. Isabella always liked that; she'd been used to William spoiling her. Isabella now had the companionship she so craved. Together she felt, they them formed a circle, a circle she could be the centre of. If Isabella ever loved anybody it was Isabella.

Isabella also now had people to do her bidding. First, there was Jenifer, who, whilst railing against her enslavement to her mother as much as reasonably possible was also mindful of their financial indebtedness. Although the finance for The Saucy Cod had been, to all appearances, freely given, Jenifer's attendance on her mother was the way the debt was to be repaid and Jenifer knew it.

In later life, Jenifer's burden was relieved somewhat as a Young Kenver took over the mantle, although he did it with a more willing heart than his mother, for Kenver was extremely fond of his grandmother as she of him. It seemed that, in so many ways, Young Kenver resembled his maternal grandparents rather than his parents. He certainly didn't seem to follow his namesake, Kenver Trescott.

Kenver was always visiting his grandmother, running little errands for Isabella and, as he grew older, undertaking odd jobs as they came along. He would sit long hours with her, giving Isabella companionship and, in her latter years, as her eyesight faded, or so she said, would read to her. Jenifer, ever cynical towards her mother, always thought this a ruse, to gain yet more attention.

Kenver, 'Young Kenver' as Isabella always referred to him, doted on his grandmother. It helped, of course, that she provided him with a permanent supply of little treats. She bought his first roller skates, his first bicycle, his first car, in fact, all his wheels. It was strange really, Kenver had so many wheels and yet he was a boy who never rolled very far.

Even after death Isabella looked after him, leaving Kenver her house and a sufficient sum for him to maintain both it and himself. Jenifer, in particular, although Allan also, would often worry as to how the boy, now a man, would develop, never having wanted for anything.

Kenver didn't show any interest in business; certainly not the family business. Isabella had brought him up that way. She'd always viewed him as developing into more gentlemanly ways, following on from his grandfather William, which was why, in part, she'd funded his private education at a school in the city.

Louise could have actually afforded to have sent Kenver to a 'better' school still, one with a name. There were, certainly, still enough funds in the pot but that would have meant Kenver having to board and be away all term. At those times, Isabella wouldn't have been the centre of someone's attention, now that William was no longer around and Jenifer, as Isabella knew, was only paying lip service. Young Kenver, as William's replacement, needed to be kept close.

So, Isabella reached a compromise with herself and Kenver was enrolled in the public school in the city, as a day pupil. The fact that it put extra pressure on Allan, ferrying the boy to and fro between home and the nearest public transport was irrelevant to Isabella; it wasn't her concern.

Jenifer, for all her education, had joined Allan in the business when they relocated to Cornwall and the business grew. They set great store by the fact that they used only Cornish potatoes, Cornish fish and Cornish beer for the batter. It was a novel concept in its time, almost futuristic. More importantly, it worked.

The marketing helped swell the profits as well as did the MacDonalds' dedication to business. It was a dedication that would have impressed Old Kenver himself. Jenifer, it seems, favours her grandfather. She favours him to such an extent that now, with several other properties both in Tredoch and the next town, Allan and Jenifer are restoring the Trescott family fortune, stone by literal stone.

Their main concern has always been that Young Kenver doesn't dissipate said fortune as his grandfather William had done before him for just as Jenifer favours her grandfather, so Young Kenver certainly does seem to favour his in certain ways.

On a more positive note, as we visit today, the tide appears to be on the turn. Kenver's parents never seemed to have realised that the boy's talents, latent as they've been, have lain elsewhere. The regular, though unambitious job in the nearby town, together with his inheritance, has proved more than sufficient for Kenver's modest and immediate needs and has left his mind free to follow its own course. It's certainly left him plenty of free time to explore his real talents.

Kenver, it appears, has taken to writing and has published his first book too, to some modest acclaim. That, however, 's another story, one that Young Kenver, the writer that he now is will, I'm sure will want to tell himself when he returns. I doubt he'll thank me for interfering.

He's currently in Singapore, on an impromptu holiday brought on by his mother says, well, she doesn't know what exactly. It was all so very sudden apparently which is most unusual for Kenver. He's never been known to do anything on the spur of the moment. He's not the spontaneous sort. Everything he's ever done's always been the result of careful thinking and then he runs it past himself at least twice to make sure he was correct in the first place. Anyway, I'm sure all will become clear in the fullness of time.

Whatever the reason Jenifer believes it will do the boy good to get out of Treddoch for a while. Who knows, she thinks, maybe he'll meet a nice girl, just like his father did.

In 'The Pie and Pasty Shop' Jason has by been joined by Sarah for the last hour or so. It's not that she's needed there quite that early; there's been very little for her to do for a while. She just likes being with Jason, even after all the years. Perhaps more so now.

An atmosphere of harmony fills the space as they work together with Jason baking, Sarah serving. It's a warm, inviting atmosphere, and not just from the heat of the oven. It's one that's immediately felt by customers as they enter. It's a definite invitation to purchase if ever there was one.

Next door but one, Jack has been joined by Tamsyn. The atmosphere in this establishment in no way resembles that in The Pie and Pasty Shop. It's quite the opposite in fact, for Jack has begun to resent the irritant that Tamsyn's presence brings into what he's increasingly come to see as his domain.

It isn't, of course, Jack's domain. It's Tamsyn's and Tamsyn likes to keep a regular check on her assets; all of her assets. If she knew of Lizzy's early morning shopping, Tamsyn might be inclined to start making her checks even sooner.

∞

In between the two, in The Fudge Shop, Joan and Henry serve with mechanical smiles. Neither really wants to be there, especially Joan, for whom this daily appearance is becoming an increasing chore. Joan doesn't 'do' chores.

At home, they now employ a cleaner to save Joan the burden, though, between the two of them, Joan and Henry barely raise any dust. A cleaner isn't really needed. It adds a touch of kudos though, when amongst their friends, for Joan to refer to 'their cleaner'.

In her mind, Joan would dearly love to raise this to the status of 'housekeeper' but, knowing that to be something she definitely won't get passed Henry, she leaves it parked there, in her mind. Joan has many dreams.

Joan's already longing for the end of The Season, even though this one's barely yet begun. The end's still four months away; four long, tedious months to Joan's way of thinking. To help ease her through, what Joan sees as troubled waters, she's started taking her holiday brochures to the shop. She now has quite a stack there as well as at home. For Joan they're a form of anti-depressant, helping her through this intensely difficult period.

Joan browses them between customers and whilst eating her healthier-than-though lunch. Henry usually has something from Jason. Each 'get-away' Joan's reading is becoming increasingly more exotic than the last. Like any drug addict, Joan has had to 'up' her fixes.

Henry realises that he'll soon have to start and reign in on Joan's expenditure; their funds are comfortable, not limitless. Henry's problem is, how does he tell that to Joan and still expect to live?

∞

On the quay, there's definitely a holiday feeling in the air aided by blue skies and sea, a golden sun and a bustle about the shoreline. Boats have now been stripped of their fishing gear and sport sturdy cushions instead, though not for their skippers' benefit. The cushions are there for the comfort of the trippers; the boats are getting ready to offer their half-hour rides along the ragged coast.

Boards of chalk lettering, crudely written, have been staged at strategic points to lure unsuspecting prospects to the water's edge where one of their numbers calls out the offer to hand. A trip not to be missed, is boldly touted.

Family prices are available for those with two or more children. Babies go free.

∞

At The Bakery, although the bulk of the day's trading's now over there's still a steady trickle of customers and there will be, for a while yet, given the time of year with its influx of visitors swelling the normal customer base.

The last bake of the day's been taken from the ovens and, as per normal practice, is being left to cool on wire racks for a while before being moved on towards customers' hands.

It has, though, on occasion, been known for bread to be sold whilst still very fresh if needs arise, its temperature requiring it be juggled from hand to hand until it falls into the shopping bag almost of its own volition. The Nancarrows have never allowed a little excess heat to stand in the way of a sale!

May's working out the back with Old Bill. Together they're making a start to the cleaning and tidying that signals the beginning of the end of the day's trading for them. Once things are a bit tidier May'll start preparing their lunch.

They always have a cooked lunch, the three of them, winter and summer alike, often a roast. To their minds, The Twins feel that this way they can be certain that Bill's had at least one good meal in the day. They tend to forget, of course, that they've been feeding him since first light. There's an egg and bacon sandwich with a cup of tea, just as soon he arrives. Sets them up for the day, to The Twins way of thinking.

After that, during the morning, Bill has at least a couple of saffron buns foisted upon him with his coffees. It's little wonder that when he does go home Bill wants very little else to eat. A snack of an evening's more than sufficient; he's almost glad of a break from eating.

The Twins worry as to what Bill does for food on a Sunday, when The Bakery's closed. Bill never says and The Twins do their best not to interfere. It doesn't stop them worrying though.

April Nancarrow is currently serving an Old Lady of even more advancing years than herself. The woman, now a widow, lives slightly inland, 'up the valley', on the very edge of village habitation. There, a few houses huddle together on either side of the lane that snakes alongside the river, seemingly for their mutual comfort and protection. Bunched together as they are, they're almost a hamlet in their own right.

The Old Lady's a widow now and has been for a couple of years. She's found it difficult, adjusting to being just one, after over forty years of being half of a two; it's the loneliness that affects her the most. The house has become quite hollow in its emptiness, the dinner table too quiet, the double bed too wide. Evenings, she finds, are her worst time; the winter ones even more so.

In days gone by she'd have come into the village probably three times a week at the most. These days, it's become a daily expedition but more for the companionship than the shopping experience. She stays as long as she can, keen to find almost anyone to talk with. It's a bit of a long walk, especially if it's wet but she doesn't mind; in fact, she quite enjoys the exercise, it helps take her mind off of her situation.

She ought to move closer to the centre The Old Lady's beginning to think, rather like her friend Alice has done. Alice, a widow like herself, craves company too; she visits the General Store some three or four times a day for her purchases. She could, of course, do her shopping all in one go but how would she spend the rest of her time.

The General Store fulfils many functions in Treddoch.


The Old Lady's leaning, conspiratorially it might seem to the casual observer. Her straw-hatted head, the hat a defence against the day, is tilted slightly forward, across the counter towards April. She's already checked around her to see if anyone might be listening before she begins speaking, which only adds somewhat to the aura of mystery.

The Old Lady, it should be noted is paying for her purchase as much with an exchange of vital information as she is with cash.

Whilst the inclination of her body and furtive glances around suggest a certain amount of privacy in the transaction, regrettably, the volume of her voice says otherwise. Unfortunately, the Old Lady's beginning to grow a little deaf with age, hence the reason she's leaning forward across the counter. It's not so much to maintain the confidence but rather, all the better for her to hear what April might be saying to her. She's also tending to speak a little more loudly these days than would be normal; purely a side-effect of her condition.

"Mrs Gormley; well, you'll never guess," says The Old Lady, beginning the conversation, both hands clutching her handbag as she rests it on the counter in front of her. Her shopping bag's on the floor beside her.

To be fair to April, she can't guess, not with such scant information so far imparted, but April's patient, she knows the Old Lady well, a regular customer from her father's day. April knows more information will be forthcoming fairly soon; the Old Lady won't be able to contain herself, not if she's gossip to share. She'll have to tell someone.

For her part, the Old Lady knows the Nancarrow twins to be good listeners. She can be confident too that information passing through the Bakery's hands will be disseminated pretty quickly to much of the remainder of the village. The Bakery's the perfect hub for this; 'Gossip Central' as some locals are wont to refer to it.

April, as always, isn't disappointed with the wait, patience brings its own rewards.

"Lives opposite me, two doors down so I can't help but notice," The Old Lady continues. The fact that the Old Lady spends a good part of her day looking out from her front window isn't mentioned in the telling. There's no need though, April's well aware of the background detail.

"I knew there'd be trouble just as soon as that Fred of hers took that job. Just knew there'd be trouble," and she shakes her head to emphasise the point. "You can't blame him though," she continues, "not really. He needs a break, poor soul. Very demanding woman that Mrs. Gormley, as you know. Very demanding."

April nods in understanding. She knows of Mrs. Gormley demanding ways, as does most of Treddoch. They all feel a certain sympathy for Fred.

"Away all week," continues the Old Lady, "in that big lorry of his. Monday morning gone prompt, bag and flask in hand. You can see, he almost has a spring in his step. Not back till Friday afternoon, late. Late as possible if you ask me. It was only to be expected though, only to be expected. I'm not surprised," and she shakes her head again at her thoughts.

April nods again, there's no need for words. April fully understands where the conversation's leading. She's not surprised either. It definitely was to be expected, sooner or later, especially with Mrs Gormley, a large, well-rounded woman of both face and figure. She's known throughout the village for her considerable and voracious appetite; her husband, Fred, a slight and slender man, was never seemingly built for the task.

"You'll never guess who she's taken up with though. Never guess," continues the Old Lady, still clutching her bag with a fearsome grip.

April shakes her head negatively, a questioning look on her face, her brain rapidly running through a list of possible contenders for the post.

"Well, I'll tell you, it's the Coal Man of all people, would you believe?"

"Never!" Now April truly is surprised, her eyes wide; stunned would probably be a better description. April's so stunned in fact that she adds a saffron bun to the Old Lady's order, completely free of charge, an event rarer than a total solar eclipse, (though she won't tell May what she's done). The gossip's worth it and it comes from a trusted source. It is, April feels, a fair exchange.

Of all the possible contenders that have been flashing through her mind as the story unfolded April definitely wasn't expecting the Coal Man to figure in it. On further reflection though, April certainly does believe, now that she's been told, for the Coal Man too has a reputation that precedes him.

Over time he's fathered more than one offspring in the surrounding area, or so it's rumoured. On due consideration and knowing Mrs. Gormley, it would need to be a man of considerable energy and stamina, as well as inclination. "Yes," April thinks, on closer consideration, "the Coal Man certainly fits the bill."

"Are you sure?" though even April wonders why she's questioning the Old Lady's observations.

"True as God's my witness," confirms the Old Lady, a committed chapel-goer of long years. "He's there every week; Wednesday afternoons, regular as clockwork. Nobody can be having that much coal delivered. Not every week. And this time of year too!"

April nods again. There's no refuting such perfect logic. Who indeed, in Treddoch, buys coal so regularly in the middle of summer, except The Bakery itself.

Still reeling from the information, "I only hope she makes him wash first" is April's only retort.

The Twins are fastidious; they can't abide dirty sheets.

∞

The last body, almost certainly, to discharge itself from bed this morning, as indeed most mornings, belongs to Rockabilly Joe, a recent addition to the village and an import outside of the more regular mould of middle-class retirees.

Rockabilly falls into that group lovingly referred to as 'eccentrics'. Given that Treddoch, hidden away as it is, seems to have been something of a magnet for eccentrics, oddities, curiosities and the dysfunctional over the centuries though, has meant the addition of a further one caused little stir when Rockabilly arrived. He fitted in extremely well from the very start.

'Rockabilly Joe', a former rock star and bon viveur, is now a rather more serious, sober, reclusive character than previous though still with a dress sense somewhat particular. It's the remnant of his stage act which, over the years, has grown to become part of his persona. Even his name's a leftover.

Rockabilly, now in his mid-thirties, is tall, slim and with a head thatched with a mane of flowing blonde hair, which, when out of the house, is topped with the addition of a stovepipe hat, the sort that Brunel would have been proud of. Unlike Brunel though, who had need of the extra inches the hat provided, Rockabilly's one only serves to cause him to look something like a pencil, with a rubber on top.

The outfit is finally finished off with a frock coat that extends towards his knees and partially covers his habitually worn blue jeans, the hallmark of a rocker.

From a distance, and at first glance, Rockabilly's often been mistaken for an undertaker, albeit a somewhat unkempt one, given his hair. Closer inspection though confirms that first impressions were correct. Rockabilly's just another idiosyncratic individual who's arrived in Treddoch with a desire to escape from whatever or wherever. This seems to be the common denominator amongst all the newcomers though there isn't a type that the village hasn't seen in its time.

Rockabilly is also single. Housekeeping never figures large in his daily routine which is why, as we visit today, as with most of his days in fact, around lunchtime, generally about twelve-thirty, you'll see him charging down the path from home to village, hair and frock coat flying out behind him as he strides purposely forward.

His hat only remains in place by the combination of a miracle and the occasional firm grip, though it's always ready to be doffed should he greet a female acquaintance in his passing. If nothing else, Rockabilly's a gentleman. The female element of Treddoch is, by and large, all very captivated by him, with some of its members being, perhaps, particularly more so than others.

> Rose is one of the 'more so' cluster. She's an acquaintance of Rockabilly's since he set first foot in the village, although Rose has always harboured secret ambitions of being raised higher in Rockabilly's affections than merely 'acquaintance'.
>
> Rose was a great fan of Rockabilly's long before he moved into Treddoch, in the days when he was at the height of his fame. She still retains all his old recordings which she cherishes, almost as much as she cherishes her association with the man himself.
>
> Like so many of the village mothers, Rose used to undertake her shopping once she'd left the children at school, first thing of a morning. Lately, though, she's changed the habits of part of a lifetime and now tends to do her shopping around lunchtime, the time Rockabilly usually makes his entrance. It's probably nothing more than a coincidence; no one should read any more into it than that.

Rockabilly meets Rose just shy of the General Store. This morning she's certainly dressed for the day, wearing a strappy sundress of a floral print that's as bright as the daylight itself and a smart pair of heeled sandals. She also seems to be wearing an extra touch of make-up, certainly more so than might be considered usual for a normal weekday.

Rockabilly lifts his hat and kisses her, in greeting, chastely on the cheek, his left hand lightly on her waist. For Rose, chaste as the kiss is it's still sufficient to stir a well of warmth that soon courses through her, heading upwards, towards her face. She hopes she doesn't blush; not this time.

"Morning Rose. You're looking very summery today; very pretty dress. It suits you, I must say." All this is said with a charm that's part of his normal conversation and are the sort of comments that only someone with Rockabilly's charisma would dare attempt and be successful with.

"Thank you," the blush does start, "and afternoon, I think you mean," Rose replies, her head held to one side, a little coquettishly. Her moss green eyes now boast a gleam that hadn't been there before Rockabilly's arrival, as she looks up towards him, her head tilted slightly back.

"Where do the mornings go?" and Rockabilly unnecessarily consults his watch, knowing full well, already, what time of day it is and where his morning has gone, as does Rose.

"I suppose you haven't long been up," Rose retorts, instantly conjuring up a mental vision of Rockabilly languishing much of the morning in bed, preferably naked to her way of thinking. Ideally, in her imagining, Rose would be lying at his side; a Rose entwined. Given the chance, she thinks, even half a chance, momentarily casting her married status to one side as she holds fast to her dream.

Rose's isn't a loveless marriage by any means, nor an unhappy one. Far from it, in fact, but it is a marriage all the same and a marriage a few years in. It's become a relationship that has settled down into a steady routine, which translates to Rose, at the moment, as being dull, rather than of contentment as it might do to others.

To Rose's mind the sparkle that had once been, no longer is. It went by way of everyday life with all the mind-numbing monotony Rose sees therein contained. The monotony of shopping and washing, of cleaning and cooking, of fetching and carrying, of lifting and shifting. The monotony of looking after little ones and a big one too, the latter sometimes seeming to be harder than the former.

Romance, to Rose's current state of thinking, seems to have long fled and been replaced by a mortgage, electricity bills, water bills, telephone bills and, well, bills in general. That Cinderella moment, in the time before marriage, has now been replaced by the mundane of everyday life.

Rose no longer feels she's the centre of somebody's attention though she still dearly wants to be. Rockabilly's able to help fill that role, in some small way. He even noticed her dress, didn't he? Her husband used to, once.

The slightest of sighs escapes Rose which she can only hope that Rockabilly doesn't notice. It wouldn't matter though if he did for Rockabilly's far too much a gentleman to comment and, anyway, he'd appreciate the attention. Although retired, his vanity can still be stirred; Rockabilly's a performer at heart.

'Rockabilly Joe', his real name long ago blasted to the Four Winds by the strident sounds from his Stratocaster, is not, as is noted, an early riser. Should he ever need to work, though ongoing royalties from his past recordings suggest this isn't going to be a necessity, Rockabilly would never find a job at The Bakery.

Rockabilly, having surfaced late, shaves, showers and takes a modest breakfast. It has to be modest for Rockabilly's the sort of singleton who keeps a thin larder. Cereal, milk, ingredients for tea or coffee is about the sum of it unless it's a good day, when there may be a packet of chocolate digestives lurking in the dark recess of a kitchen cupboard.

Rockabilly's usual routine of a days is to head for the village centre to start with, which is where he fell in with Rose, collect his newspaper, then consider where he's going to eat which can be a variable feast.

Having settled in Treddoch, he believes for life, Rockabilly likes to spread his patronage among the eating establishments, showing no particular sign of favour. Today, his thoughts are for a pub lunch and, after saying goodbye to Rose, he heads towards The Schooner Inn for a pie and a pint. His paper's firmly under his left arm, ready to be intermittently read whilst eating and chatting.

Rockabilly's no longer a man in a hurry, his days are his own now. He has more than enough time to stop and smell the roses.

> Rockabilly lives in the large house on the promontory, built long ago for a local captain of industry, in the days when pilchard fishing was at its height and tourism, as an industry, was in its infancy.
>
> It's a substantial house with panoramic windows, something unheard of till then in a village built in the days when glass cost serious money. The house was built both to demonstrate the gentleman's wealth and position in

society in general and the village in particular.

It also served him as a watchtower for, from there, he could look out to sea and watch the boats as they scooped his catch or back inland to where his warehouse was and see the women packing his pilchards into their barrels.

All had worked well until the pilchards left. When they did so too did the entrepreneur, to more lucrative fishing grounds, much like The Property Developer had in more recent times.

The house has changed hands on a regular basis since then. Owners have come and gone with amazing frequency. They come when they first see the beauty of its position, views to almost beyond the horizon, cliff path walks right outside their door, a craggy landscape to the shore below.

They go though, when they realise it can become a lonely spot too. This can be especially so come a wild, wet and windy November evening, lost in a pit of coal dark. At such times not even the twinkle of a solitary star is able to break through and a fearsome sou'-westerly, bent on destruction, rampages and rants its wrath, bowing as much as it can before it.

In these circumstances, it soon becomes a seemingly long walk from the village, heads down against the wind. It's especially so when loaded with bags of shopping, when needing to fetch the odd pint of milk, or when goods need to be delivered and no one wants to deliver them that far.

The postman can be their only visitor on some occasions and even he doesn't come every day it's been noted. Some owners have held the view that he keeps the post over till the following day, to save the excessive walk.

For Rockabilly the house is a gift. It's unlikely that he'll be leaving any time soon for, not only to his mind, is the place so utterly peaceful, so utterly beautiful but, and most importantly, it looks out west, home to where his dream lives.

Where previous owners hated the storms and gales the West Wind brings, Rockabilly adores them, wants to be out in them, to feel them. They still have a bond, Rockabilly and the West Wind. It goes way back. The house on the promontory could have been built with Rockabilly in mind; it has just stood and waited patiently for his arrival.

The house also suits his mood, away from the crowds that had once been so much part of his life and now aren't.

There had been a wife, once, and a normal job, for a short while, after leaving school, but that was a long, long time ago and in Rockabilly's mind now, a world away.

They had married young, probably, on reflection, too young. It had all seemed so romantic at the time but very soon, the music had come along. It was all a bit informal at first, a bit amateurish but then came The Band, and with The Band the fame. Like so many in his industry at the time it all came down to the money and the flesh.

There was a lot of both, especially the flesh and Rockabilly chased them with an equal passion. He couldn't resist the adulation of the fans and the continual frequency with which the female section threw their knickers in his direction.

The wife of his youth rapidly disappeared into the background chaff. There were no children to complicate matters, not even a goldfish to fight over, for custody. Anyway, Rockabilly didn't want to fight he just wanted to play his music and be adored. The break was as clean as it was inevitable. Rockabilly's life took on one tack, his wife's another, with a sufficient, financial payment to ease her pain.

Sex, drugs, rock 'n' roll soon became Rockabilly's life, especially the sex and the rock 'n' roll. The drugs were a bonus, for a time, until he tired of them that is and walked. He was more fortunate than many of his compatriots who either couldn't or wouldn't.

Now, as we visit, and still only in his late thirties, Rockabilly is technically retired. Life retired him. The music scene retired him. Mostly though, his fans retired him for he no longer writes the music he once wrote and whilst this music, now so very different from what he'd previously written, suits Rockabilly, it no longer suits them. They haven't been enamoured with the change.

Fortunately, Rockabilly was in a position not to need to bother. He was able to do what he wanted to do, not need to do for he's been a little more than a one-hit-wonder. There've been several hits in fact and a few albums, all well received, which is how Rockabilly can afford the large house on the promontory, linked to the village by little more than a tarmacked track and eat out most every lunchtime without the need for work.

> Rockabilly fell in love with the West Wind when coming to the height of his fame. Alcohol, in copious quantities, became too heady a mix to mentally cope with when added to the already existing baseload of sex, drugs, and rock'n'roll. The inner machinations of his brain took on a life of their own.
>
> Rockabilly had found her one night, this mythical lover, this woman of air and mind, after a concert early in his career, when he went out walking. Her gusts billowed his hair, taking away his original hat, leaving the wet to streak his face and clothes and run into his shoes.
>
> The Wind abused him and Rockabilly loved it. The more

she abused, the more he loved. He wrote his music for her; wild music, music that matched her wilder moments. She stirred him, enthused him, motivated him. It was the West Wind that inspired his best works, gave him hit songs, filled his bank account.

Women came and went, have come and gone, still come and go, on occasion. Only the West Wind, and now her replacement, the dream-in-waiting, find a consistency in his heart.

None of the other Winds ever compared to her in Rockabilly's mind. At the time she was his one true and only love, however unreal. His former wife had never scaled such heights in his affection.

Rockabilly could have chosen any of the four sisters for his inspiration and attention. They all have their individual qualities after all; all are unique in their separate ways.

The North Wind though, Rockabilly found cold and lifeless, her body the texture of dead flesh. He couldn't bear her touch against his skin; he still can't. When she appears he wants to run, to hide, keep a safe, sound distance. Rockabilly dismissed her considerations immediately.

Similarly with the East Wind, with her bleak eyes and hooked nose, bitter and cruel in both spirit and face. The East Wind's a spiteful wind. Rockabilly always felt that she'd soon eat through him, given the chance.

Now the South Wind, ah! the South Wind. The South Wind was a different matter. Rockabilly could easily have fallen for the South Wind with her glass dark hair and warm, urgent fingers that always made him tingle when she languidly ran them over his body and lightly ruffled the flows of his hair. He loved those warm caresses which could take him to another plane, leave him relaxed to the point of being utterly lethargic.

When all were tested though it was the West Wind that stole Rockabilly's heart without even trying. She stole it completely, utterly, totally. Stole it without question, without compensation.

It was a love at first sight for Rockabilly and this West Wind, a wind with warm, soft moments of gentle quiet, tender at times but interspersed on a sudden, on an impulse, with fits of rage, outbursts of temper that would threaten to blow both mind and body apart. Rockabilly found her wild and intoxicating, he was unable to resist. It's she that caught his love at the time. There could be no other for him; the rhythm of his music had followed her moods.

Rockabilly's grateful for all the West Wind has done for him. She made him; he's never forgotten her nor the debt he owes. He'd gladly, willingly sold his soul for her, bound himself to her, in perpetuity, or at least until he'd sobered and cleaned up.

She has left a legacy though, this mythical lover, this West Wind. Although the Wind herself was just a fantasy, Rockabilly knows, in his heart, that somewhere, out there, to the west lies the woman of his dreams; the real woman. It's all a matter of waiting for her arrival. His flirtation with the West Wind was but a precursor.

Rockabilly had the sense to realise that he couldn't continue at the pace he'd originally set for himself, not forever. Both the pace and the drugs were eating into him, not to mention the alcohol. He wouldn't last much longer if he didn't change, they'd see to that. They were beginning to affect him, and anyway, he was starting to tire of all that flesh. He'd gorged long enough, drunk too deep and all in too short a time. There'd already been more than enough for one man's life.

So Rockabilly changed. He quit the drugs completely and reduced the alcohol and the women to more manageable proportions.

As he changed his life, so too, he changed his music. The new music was no longer harsh and baying but became soft and gentle; his songs became songs of love, not hate. It had all begun as music to calm the West Wind's wrath, to ease her pain but as Rockabilly morphed and regained some semblance of normalcy so did his fantasies.

The personified West Wind was returned to what she was, just that, whilst he transferred his affections to the dream young woman he now thinks of. He visualises her, standing on some distant headland, somewhere far out to the west. He sees her cloak streaking out behind her as does her long flowing hair which is the epitome of the evening sun as it sinks her way. On her head a thousand shades of reds merge, in turn, with blacks of equal number, colours that, outside of the natural world, only Johnny's palette can emulate.

So Rockabilly began to write his new songs but now for her, this woman of his dreams. This is how he's come to lose his fan base, but subsequently discovered a level of contentment and peace for his new self in this house on the promontory, above the little harbour that's Treddoch.

At about the same time that Rose is trifling with Rockabilly Joe, Johnny's beginning to stir from a distraught sleep in his chair. Almost automatically, he rubs his knuckles across the top of an itching chest where Bastet's scored him earlier this morning as he lay in his alcoholic coma.

When Johnny had slumped into his chair it was for the clear and simple purpose of clearing a throbbing head. Unexpectedly though, the sheer depth of slumber that he'd fallen into has exposed him to a strange amalgam of visions and images. It's been a bizarre mixture, even for an artist like Johnny, someone whose always been prepared to paint on a wider canvas than his contemporaries in order to express himself.

As much as Johnny can recall of these images, there was a cat, definitely, a cat. He most certainly remembers there being a cat if only because of the eyes. Yes, eyes he recalls. That's it, eyes. It's not so much the cat itself but its eyes that Johnny recalls, although these weren't any old eyes, even for a cat.

They certainly weren't eyes as he might normally expect eyes to be, that was for sure. These were more akin to black holes than anything for they drew him ever towards them no matter how much he tried to resist. He couldn't turn his head and look away.

Stranger still, they were there at the end of a tunnel, a tunnel formed from a gauntlet of old women with severely elongated, pointing fingers that jabbed at him as he was drawn through. What was even more bizarre still, certainly to Johnny's remembering, was that there'd also been aggressive-looking paintbrushes that had, somehow, become incarnate.

They'd chased and hounded him, these brushes, pushing him through the gauntlet, continually stabbing their sharper ends into his back, nagging him as they prodded, their bristles pointedly bare for the want of paints. On and on they'd pushed, down through the gauntlet, ever onwards, towards the eyes.

Or had that been the cat, doing the prodding, Johnny wonders as he rubs his chest again. Images and memories have definitely blurred since their feverish conceptions. Whichever way, of looking though, Bastet figures prominently in the mix. She's had a starring role for one of such diminutive stature. Clearly, The Cat has left a lasting impression on Johnny, in more ways than one.

Johnny's finding the point of waking-up to be little easier than the sleep itself though. Shaking off the slumber doesn't do much to ease his situation for whatever's been in his mind whilst he had slept has now been released in the wakening. It hovers there, hanging in the air around him, wraith-like. It may be lacking in form or substance but it's there, never-the-less. Johnny can feel its presence.

"Where am I?" asks Johnny of no one in particular. It's fired merely at the space before him, so Johnny's somewhat startled when he receives a response.

"Nowhere and you never will be, unless it's at the bottom of the harbour, like your father. Dead drunk," the voice of air, replies. "That's your future, Johnny." Though it's the height of summer, such a thought sends a winter's chill through Johnny's bones. Death, he feels, doesn't become him, certainly not yet.

"I *can* do better," he half insists to the disembodied voice, although he's not quite convinced himself as is evidenced by the hint of caution in his response.

"No, you can't. You never could. Let's face it, Johnny, you've never even tried. 'Could do better'! 'Must try harder!' Ring any bells, Johnny? Do they bring back any memories?"

Images of old school reports float past Johnny's view. The truth of the commentary stings, as if he's hearing it for the first time though of course, he's not. He's just managed to keep it suppressed, buried all this while. Nothing stays imprisoned forever though; everything's released at some point, if only by death.

Truth and reality, held bound for so long, have escaped from Johnny this morning and are rapidly leading to remorse; remorse for many things but, especially, for time lost. It's also a remorse not only for time lost in general but of time lost for Abi in particular; especially for Abi and how he's treated her. It's she that's carried them so far, he knows full well; Johnny's contribution has never passed zero.

He thinks of all those early protestations of his, none of which have ever come to fruition. She's deserved better than him, he's always known it. This really is a sober and sobering moment for Johnny. He can't remember the last time, if ever there was one, that reality has hit him like its hitting him this morning. His past's finally beginning to weigh on his conscience.

It's also lunchtime, as the kitchen clock and his stomach both pointedly tell. Johnny does indeed feel a hunger, but he's uncertain if it's to do with the fact that he's not eaten since before ambling to the pub last night or the result of an empty soul? It's something of both most likely.

Nourishing the first is easy. Johnny makes a cheese and pickle sandwich which is normally, a great favourite of his. It's worth noting that Johnny's culinary expectations have always been of limited extent. This time, though, and contrary to normal practice, he chews somewhat automatically and without satisfaction, his mind's ruminating more on the images and thoughts still cascading through his head. There are still those eyes; they're compelling. They're holding him transfixed. Fortunately for Johnny, he hasn't completely lost all of his artistic sensibility to the ale.

The sandwich, now finished, is merely filling a hole in his stomach. Concrete would serve much the same purpose.

Nourishing the second of his two hungers is less easy to achieve. To start with, the solution isn't as immediately obvious as a buttering a slice of bread to accompany a lump of cheese.

Without a doubt, though, there's definitely something starting to gnaw at his innards, like a rat at a piece of rope, and it's demanding to be fed too. Whatever it is, this time, it's not going away and alcohol won't mask it anymore; Johnny knows that.

His stomach filled and with a fresh cup of tea in hand, Johnny shaves and showers, before looking for some clean clothes. It's only at this point that he sees the random spread of paintings on the bed.

Did he really paint them? Is that Abi? She really was beautiful, wasn't she? She still is, of course, when he pauses to think of her, something he realises hasn't done for a long time. Had he really captured her so well or was she, is she, just a good model. Perhaps a bit of both. They had been so good together, hadn't they? Once. He thinks fondly of her, his Abi, the first time in many a long year.

Johnny's school reports had consistently stated, 'must try harder', 'could do better', as his conscience has only now reminded him. The comments were true of course, even in those days and Abi has deserved better, deserves better; much better in fact. Johnny knows this. The problem's been that Johnny's just never faced up to it. Drinking to exhaustion on a regular and recurring basis has always seemed so much easier and, of course, much more fun; or so he's thought till now.

Johnny fingers the paintings, shuffling them around, looking at them intently from whichever angle. He sees what can be, if only he can get off his backside and 'try harder', It can't be that tough surely. Others have done it. Clearly, it's finally time for him to grow up; he can't be a lad forever. He thinks again of his father, visualising him lying there, entombed. Stone cold, stone dead. These days, just stone.

Johnny knows he could do better, can do better; he believes it. The evidence is here, in the paintings. It's imperative, he *must* do better. Last night really has to be the past and forever.

Johnny no longer has a choice.

It's now that he sees it, as he sits there brooding over paintings of long ago. There's an enlightenment of truly Damascan dimensions which he can only attribute, somehow to that cat. That cat again.

"Bloody Cat!"

Is it The Cat, though? Who knows? Johnny is certainly beginning to think this way; that she's having some influence over him, and he's sober now. Is it the paintings spread before him perhaps? Johnny can't but help see what he's capable of. Or is it Abi? Not just how beautiful she is there as she looks back at him but the realisation of just how much he owes to her, as Rockabilly believes he owes the West Wind.

Maybe, ultimately, it's nothing more than time for change, for change for Johnny is certainly long overdue. Whatever the reason, to Johnny's mind Bastet somehow seems to be The Catalyst.

That's it, as he leaps from the bed; The Cat. The eyes. Mesmeric. He has to paint them. No, not just paint, not merely paint. He needs to capture them. Reflect them on canvas just as he saw them in those early hours.

"Bloody Cat!" Johnny mutters again and storms into the garden to raid the dilapidated shed, the roof of which he's long forgotten to fix, flinging junk to either side, making the mess that already is, grow by increasing amounts.

Finally, there, under everything, is what he's seeking. A box. A large, tin box. No wonder it's at the bottom of everything. How long's it been since it last saw the light of day. Too long, that's abundantly clear, judging by the condition he finds it in.

Johnny makes the token, but ineffectual gesture, of blowing dust and webs away before heaving the box free and out into open light, lifting the lid with a feeling bordering on trepidation.

The contents shrink back. They've been used to the dark so long, daylight frightens them. Everything's still there, just as it was left.

"Excellent! Excellent!"

Renewed of purpose, filled with fresh vigour and now, fully armed, Johnny strides off towards the harbour in search of Bastet, the unlikeliest of Muses. The image of her eyes is still raging through his mind with all the intensity of a bush fire in full burn.

At about the same time that Johnny's leaving home, Bastet's in the garden to the rear of Molly's cottage, on the boundary where Molly's careful cultivation rises steadily to meet the scrub and outcropped rock that are the cliffs beyond.

She's toying with a terrified mouse. It's not that The Cat's hungry, as her still partially full food bowl bares testament. No, it's purely for her own personal amusement and sadistic pleasure, a game to pass the time until something more interesting comes along, like a freshly prepared bowl of food.

Bastet disdains to eat anything that's been left long enough to even teeter on the edge of stale. The food in her bowl has now reached that stage and is, in Bastet's very partisan opinion, fit only for flies. The flies, for their part, relish the banquet offered and would be grateful for Bastet's offering, if gratitude was within their remit.

The mouse, too petrified to squeak, heart thumping, legs pounding, focuses to dash and dodge every which way there is in a futile attempt to escape its tormentor. Just when it thinks it has, a perfect paw, trimmed with razor-sharp claws, comes down upon it, not severe enough to do any damage, just enough to corral it and continue the sport. Like all hunting, it can be fun unless you're the one being hunted.

This, though, must be the mouse's lucky day for Bastet, on the spur, lets it free. Whether it's the heat of the midday sun, which doesn't usually affect her, the onset of boredom with the exercise, or time to move on to other things which she senses to be happening, she doesn't really know.

Whichever it is, The Cat, at moment's notice, leaves a bewildered but eternally thankful mouse and saunters back to the cottage front and collapses in the shade of Molly's latticed porch. She stretches out a languid paw and waits.

The mouse, without need of help or encouragement, scuttles back, full tilt, to hide in the comparative safety of the nearby undergrowth which it now realises, it should never have left in the first instance and promises itself it never will again so long as it lives. It hopes, the lesson learned, means it will now live longer than appeared only moments ago.

# Afternoon

The afternoon isn't particularly noteworthy in the village day, unlike nine o'clock or even lunchtime. The afternoon is just the middle of somewhere. It lacks the significance of being either a beginning or an end.

It's not a period to record especially, for both the pace and tone have already been set in general terms and will continue at steady drip till teatime. Only then will the rhythm of the day alter.

Visitors are still arriving, just as others are beginning to leave though some of the latter are leaving less willingly perhaps than others. The problem for these visitors is that their allotted time in the car park, pre-booked as it is, is rapidly hastening towards its end, and, in consequence, demands a quick and forced evacuation.

"I told you to put more money in the machine, didn't I? Now we've got to rush." The warmth of the day, not conducive to rushing, is as good an agent as any to kick-start a family argument.

"I thought it'd be enough. We can always come back another day." By way of compromise and appeasement.

"I don't want to come back another day. I'd have liked to have stayed longer today." In petulance. She would have stamped her foot if they hadn't have been walking.

"Well, you should have said you wanted to stay longer." In exasperation.

"I did. You just ignored me. As usual." The final volley. Unanswerable.

He can't argue back any longer; He's absolutely no idea as to whether She said it or not or whether He ignored Her or not. The fact She's adamant means, to Her mind, She's correct. There's no point in quarrelling further as the passing of years has taught Him; He's found it best just to accept His lot.

They continue their hastened walk, the silence of their conversation overwhelming.

Sadly, the situation won't be improved when they reach their car either, for the temperatures inside are set to make Hell the more appealing and can only serve to exacerbate an already poisonous situation.

This state-of-affairs will remain for a couple of hours until a beneficial combination of food and drink will calm and soothe fretted nerves. If all won't exactly be forgotten, it will certainly be forgiven.


They mish-mash with themselves, these visitors, and with the residents too as groups skirt groups, all moving every which way through the streets; only rarely ever in a straight line. They check shop windows, record precious moments, taking photographs they're unlikely to ever view again and pause to watch the Maypole Dancing that's about to take place on the patch of ground considered to be the village centre.

They also browse the two or three stalls positioned raggedly to one side of the entertainment, attaching themselves like limpets to the main attraction, each eager to raise funds for their particular activity.

This year they're collecting for the Christmas Lights, the upcoming Folk Festival and a Community Bus. Generally speaking, each stall is selling someone else's left-overs, and cakes. There's always cakes. The cakes, at least, are fresh.

∞

The Maypole's been in place since lunchtime, brought from the school by The Caretaker, just as he's done these many years. He doesn't need any instruction; he knows what to do if only because of the repetition. Maypole dancing's a time-honoured tradition, in Treddoch on Solstice Day, comparable with that of May Day.

Like so many traditions, so with this one, the timing and reasoning for its beginnings are lost to history but it is a tradition and must, therefore, be duly honoured as is its right.

The children from the 'top' class will be dancing, just as The Caretaker himself once did in a time now past. His son danced too, though it seems unlikely, certainly, given how things stand at the moment domestically, that his grandson ever will.

Molly too remembers dancing, when Mr. Trengrouse was Headmaster. He's been dead these ten years Molly reflects and there's been another occupant in his old office between his and Molly's reigns.

Molly had always been very fond of Mr. Trengrouse, a father figure to all the children and something of an inspiration to Molly in particular.

He'd spotted her intellectual prowess at an early age and encouraged Molly to develop it, feeding her literature she would never otherwise have digested, coming from a fishing family as she does, a family where, historically, education had been good but rudimentary.

Mr. Trengrouse had helped lift Molly's to another level, for which her parents were eternally grateful, his attention to their only daughter duly noted. They'd attended his funeral as a mark of respect.

Leaving school after dinner, the children have walked down in a more stylised formation than they'll be doing later, when the school day ends. Now though, they are being supervised by 'Miss' herself and are, accordingly, all on their best behaviour, all that is except for a couple of boys at the back who have to be brought into line, quite literally, one or two times.

'Growing pains', her mother would call them. It'll soon change, Molly reflects, come next term and secondary school. They'll be just two little fish in a big, big sea then. Molly can still recall such feelings. She'd felt a very small fish indeed and for quite some time.

As Molly's academic abilities had developed ahead of most of her peers, Molly came to feel increasingly isolated; something of an island. It's a feeling she's never been able to fully shake off, even to this day.

As well as the maypole the caretaker's also taken the School's gramophone along, together with its external speaker and connected the gramophone, via an extension cable that's meandering in a manner oblivious to both health and safety, to Jason's shop. Jason's kindly providing the electricity for the event, free of charge, of course.

Now, with the children in place, their backs straight, arms down by their sides, their feet together and with ribbons in hands, Molly, somewhat ceremoniously, lowers the needle, taps a right foot and momentarily waits until raucous sounds, only distantly akin to music, grind out through the speaker and give cue to the little dancers to begin their antics, skipping and hopping first this way then that, tangling and untangling as is due process with a maypole.

If some dance with two left feet, then Molly doesn't notice. They're wonderful, all of them, without exception, and they're all her children, at least for the moment. Their parents can reclaim them later but, for now, they're hers. It's such moments as this that Molly can forget her loneliness for the while.

On the periphery, an impromptu audience is suddenly assembling, all drawn by the harsh blaring of the speaker as much as by the swirl of ribbon. Curious visitors pause in their ramblings, pause in their browsing, just pause at the sight of this unexpected and generally welcome entertainment.

They mix with the few parents able to take time out to watch their offspring and the occasional local who's suddenly appeared, as they do every year at this time. It's as if they carry an alarm, pre-set from years past.

There's pride for parents, entertainment for visitors, nostalgia for many, as memories of long past childhoods resurface. Smiles spread, hands clap, feet tap and all mostly in time.

Then, when all's finished and the crowd dare think to disperse Molly calls for a reprise, just in case anybody's missed the first performance. Well, at least that's Molly's excuse.

As the music blares Johnny's reached Molly's cottage and in record time too, certainly at a speed that's, for him, a personal best for many a long while. Bastet's to be found already lounged on the doormat, shading from the afternoon sun. Supper's still some while away.

"Cat! Here!" Johnny commands of Bastet, who, under normal circumstances would at most, have raised a disdainful eye before treating such an instruction with the contempt she would ordinarily feel it deserves.

Under normal circumstances nobody, but nobody ever orders the aristocratic Bastet around, unless, of course, there's a piece of fresh fish involved. Sacrifices can be made if the rewards are sufficient! The old adage is true, even Bastet has her price.

But these aren't 'normal circumstances' for on seeing Johnny, Bastet stretches, yawns and languidly rises. She isn't going to make this too easy for him. Johnny's going to have to work for his salvation.

To Johnny's startled eyes, Bastet leisurely jumps onto the low wall and from there to the gate post, assuming a suitable pose in one fluid motion. She's always favoured a full-on view, rather than a side profile, so she gazes toward Johnny directly now, head held majestically but pointed sufficiently downwards so the two of them are lined eye to eye. Front legs parallel, paws turned slightly out, Bastet sits on her haunches, tucking her sleek tail neatly around and under her. A regal sitting.

Johnny can already feel the power emanating from The Cat's eyes as she stares at him whilst he mixes and matches colours, painting with a fluidity that belies the more usual shambolic ambling that's been his trademark of late.

The newly wetted brushes whir in his fingers as a bow might on a fiddle, a blur of wood and bristle, as colours mixed and blended in his palette flow to canvas at a speed that defies light.

Johnny's, clearly back at the top of his game.

A few visitors pause in passing to watch the artist in action, heads nodding in approval as the form takes shape, grows before them. Voices are kept to a murmur so's not to disturb the master's concentration. The transferred image seems more life-like than the sitter herself.

Photographs are taken, appreciative comments made, though not too loud. It won't matter if they are though for Johnny's totally oblivious to all around him, lost to the task at hand. He's not simply focused but absorbed, captivated, immersed, capturing that singular depth of darkness that is Bastet's eyes and transferring them to canvass without loss in the process.

Mission completed, Johnny falls back to rest against the wall of the adjoining building, exhausted mentally. He's too tired even to look at what he's accomplished.

Instinctively, The Cat, knowing the sitting to be ended, flows gracefully down to the floor, a deep rolling purr emanating from the back of her throat as she resumes her earlier position in front of Molly's door. She hopes there'll be nothing else to disturb her afternoon, though she has, of course, adored the attention of the crowd, small though she feels it was. There was a time, she remembers, when her appearance would have attracted much bigger numbers.

Embarrassed by the attention his work has caused, Johnny half-smiles, nods somewhat rigidly to the cluster around him in thanks for their appreciation, collects his belongings and leaves as hastily as he reasonably can.

Tom's timing for his return from the town's a little adrift from what he'd originally planned; his own fault entirely, as he acknowledges. His feet were to blame; it's all their fault, he reckons.

Once Tom had completed his business with the solicitor, his feet had dragged him waterward, to the town's harbour There was no way they could resist; the pull of its anchorage was far too strong and Tom's will far too weak to overrule them in such a matter. A quick stroll, a peek at the boats, a last look around was the intention they'd given.

There are still a few old faces there that Tom knows, a few, men like himself from fishing days now gone. Their numbers, like those of the fish, are on a steady decline. Each year has taken its toll, surreptitious-like, until there'll soon be none of the old brigade left at all. The younger men are continuously compelled to climb life's ladder, Tom reflects, regardless of wish.

Still, on a more positive note, Tom had felt that there were some faces, like his own, for whom fishing days, though long over, that still liked to poke around among the nets and fish boxes. They can't go out on the water anymore, but they can't keep away from its edge either. The pull's too strong, like the moon on the tides.

The warmth of the Summer's day's been an added magnet, holding them there just that bit longer than a Winter's one might have as they've ruminated on times past, talked of shoals long swum, of crab pots long empty.

Tom's enjoyed times recaptured, if only briefly, thankful for the decision his feet have made for he's no longer certain the opportunity will present itself again. In fact, Tom's thinking quite the opposite; he's been seeing too many dark clouds for such a sunny day. He feels instinctively that this will be his last Midsummer; he won't be seeing another one.

To compensate for time lost to travel and talk, especially the talk, and not wanting to cook this evening, Tom buys a pasty from Jason as he passes, heading for his cottage, pausing only to look at his harbour.

The Town's one's alright, in its way but a little too large for Tom's liking and Tom likes *this* harbour, *his* harbour. Tom knows every inch of it, every boat that there is or has been, every stone and pebble that surfaces its bottom, every bolt fixed into the wall to tie the boats tight to, leaving them no chance to slip out on a tide at whim with lack of a helmsman.

Warm pasty in hand Tom stands, contented, at peace, satisfied both with what he sees and with what he's accomplished today. He's confident that Mary would have approved. Tom's always been keen to have Mary's approbation and still is, to the end.

With a smile on his face, Tom walks through his cottage door and once out of view takes a bite from his food as one might of a last supper.

"Maybe not local born," thinks Tom, "but that boy sure knows how to cook a proper pasty."

# Early Evening

Six o'clock is something of a watershed in the village, as the more hectic pace of the daytime switches over to a slower one for the evening ahead.

The coaches have all recovered their loads, turned tail and fled *en masse*. For the most part, so too have the day-trippers who came by car. There are just a few stragglers remaining, holding on to the last, but they too can be seen meandering towards the car park, happy in general with their day by the sea, but now, a little tired. They're ready for drinks, dinner and a bit of a rest.

Holidaying can be quite tiring.

Like the visitors, many of the traders too have had enough for one day; tomorrow'll be here soon enough. Most of the shops and cafés are already closed, those that aren't soon will be. It's too early yet to be thinking of staying open for the evening trade. It'll be another month before The Season's ready for that so the traders are taking advantage of an evening at home while they can.

The Saucy Cod's, completing last orders for those wanting to take a bite away with them. Holidays aren't a time for cooking. There's enough of that the rest of the year.

Needless to say, Joan and Henry, last to open are first to close. By five-thirty, they're ready to leave, or, in Joan's case, flee. She's had sufficient of the public at large by now. Too many, too noisy and, on the whole, for Joan, too crass. The hanging sign on the inside of the door is turned pointedly from 'Open' to 'Closed', the door pulled fast, locked and bolted till tomorrow. It's the sort of tomorrow Joan would rather not see.

Home beckons to Joan; her home. It's an oasis, she likes to think; a place of peace and tranquillity. She can still remember a previous house, a long time ago now but it's still there, on the fringe of memories that will persist, despite Joan's best efforts to expunge them. That house was far too full of people, too messy and far too noisy to Joan's way of thinking. There was no quiet, no privacy, no space to call her own.

Home is now a more refined and genteel space where soft, understated music from their new and, naturally, expensive music system will enhance the ambience Joan so embraces.

Henry misses a bit of Heavy Metal himself. Unlike Jason, though, who has long lost his surfboard to time and space, Henry still keeps his old air guitar close and safe. It's the only personal thing he seems to have remaining and is his most prized possession. It's always with him, even in his darkest moments; it's something Joan can't take from him.

It may seem sad to some but it's important to Henry. It's always ready for those instants, that odd occasion, rare though they might be, when Joan's not around and he can listen to his own more spirited selection. He's paid for the system, after all, Henry tells himself. It's his to do with as he damn well pleases. In those moments of solitary, he makes it work to his bidding, remembering, of course, to always restore Joan's settings when he's finished.

This is their second Season of trading, Joan's seriously questioning whether she can face the prospect of a third but Henry, for once authoritative with her, has said she must. They'll need three years trading accounts before they can return the business to the market if they hope for a good price. Henry has lost much to Joan but not his business acumen. Joan is prepared to sacrifice a battle to win the war.

Patience closes her shop's door pretty much as the village clock chimes six though she's fairly relaxed on the exact timing. Organising herself takes time and she's in no hurry to rush home, there's no one waiting for her there. It's just an empty house, a shell of a place, despite all its elegant furnishing. It's not even a place with memories, for Charles had lived the briefest of time there before he'd died. Sometimes she thinks it all very inconsiderate of him, leaving her alone like this although she suspects Charles isn't too happy with the situation either.

As per routine, she'll sit down for an hour with her gin and tonic, looking out across the harbour and then organise their dinners, hers and the One-Eyed Dog's. It's the same routine every night, although she may alter it, fractionally, tonight she thinks, for the evening's warm and the air still.

Patience has decided to take advantage of the weather and have her drink in the garden, sitting for a while under the evening sun, gazing out across the harbour towards the sea. The dog, unwilling to be left even a few yards away, will, undoubtedly follow.

If it weren't for the loneliness it would be idyllic. She misses Charles dreadfully, though it's not something she'd admit to anyone. She has her pride and knows no-one close enough for her to talk to on that plane.

Why did he have to have been so much older than her? It hadn't seemed to matter once, but then they were both younger. The thought of him dying long before her was something she'd rarely thought about in the years past. Perhaps she hadn't wanted to, inevitable as it was going to be.

As fond of him as she is, the One-Eyed Dog can never really be a substitute for Charles. No one can.

For his part, the One-Eyed Dog's as contented as any dog can be, lying there at Patience's feet. He's very grateful to Patience.

As every night during The Season, Patience calls through the shop doorway of the Trendy Young Couple as she passes to wish them a "Goodnight," and "hope you've had a good day," together with one or two other pleasantries.

None of it's of any great consequence, it's just some gentle conversation. For all their bright and gaudy attire, their extremely lively and distinctive shop décor, Patience senses that something dark and brooding hangs over them, almost noose-like. Whatever it is, and Patience is far too polite to question, she sees that there is something blighting their young lives, preventing a couple like them, free and independent as they are, from enjoying their time as Patience feels they should be doing.

> All this conversation passes, quite literally, over the head of the One-Eyed Dog, of course, standing, as he does, uncomplainingly to heel, merely wondering what Patience's organised for dinner tonight. It's always something special; not like the dark days before the coming of Patience. A bit of steak perhaps, maybe chicken although Patience will always add rice when it's chicken. Something the vet had said once he recalls. "Mix some rice in with his diet. Not too much red meat. And make sure he has some dried food as well. Good for his teeth."
>
> Not much of a vet the One-Eyed Dog had thought at the time. The dried food he can tolerate but he's never forgiven him for adding rice to the menu.

The Trendy Young Couple are waiting to close their shop too, though, already and it's only their second Season, out of habit they wait for Patience to close first. She's a 'lovely woman', they both think; a 'proper lady', unlike some, they remember, from their past. It would be rude of them, they feel, not to wait those few minutes to speak with her as she passes. They both sense her loneliness. Despite their problem, they do at least have each other to lean on. It helps. Who does Patience have, they wonder?

The Couple usually go to the Fisherman's Loft after closing for a 'swift half' and tonight will be no exception, though, like Patience, they'll probably sit outside if they can.

With little more space behind their counter than battery hens might get, they've been cooped up inside this stuffy shop all day. In fact, after dinner, they'll probably go for a stroll over the cliffs they've already decided. It's the perfect evening for it. The village really is at its very best. They'd better take advantage of it whilst they can for, hopefully, another fifteen months and they'll be leaving; everything crossed.

Duncan has tidied his art gallery, set some new and garish landscapes on display in the window and closed his door on another day. The takings haven't been too bad and now he can head home for a beer, as bitter as himself, and a bite to eat.

How dearly he would love to be a 'proper' artist. One for whom the brushes dance and the paint flies as they whirl between palette and paper. For Duncan, attaching paint to paper is a heavy plod, slow and deliberate, each stroke painstakingly thought out. His present piece is the result of several more hours of toil than it should have needed. If only he had talent to execute it with better flair, he ponders.

How Duncan envies Johnny and how, equally, he despises Johnny for squandering his talent. The thought of Johnny wasting such talent that he would so gladly, readily, embrace constantly gnaws at him and, as he's getting older, is eating into him with increasing frequency. What he wouldn't give to have half of Johnny's talent. A quarter even. He's reached the point where he'd genuinely sell his soul, so dark has become Duncans thinking.

There's nothing much on the television that he wants to watch tonight, Duncan's already checked. He might go back to the shop later and continue his latest piece. If he's lucky, he might even get it finished so that it can go out it on sale tomorrow.

He likes to think his watercolours are improving and perhaps they are, in technique. Goodness knows he's practiced long enough, but, for all his efforts, they still lack Life. They're little more than architectural drawings, stilted as they are. Duncan has never been able to pour even a fraction of himself into his work. He knows, in his heart, that this is where his failing really lies. He was never born to be an artist as Johnny was.

John Tregear has closed the Shell Shop and is already out of the door and scurrying his way to the harbour, warned again, by Anne, to 'keep his eye on the time'. Dinner will be on the table on the stroke of seven. John knows the situation to be non-negotiable.

Still, for an hour, there's the prospect of some fresh air and possible conversation with like-minded souls, not the tourists he's spoken with all day. Not that John minds them, these tourists, for he's mindful that they fill his till and some he genuinely finds interesting in their conversation.

Very soon it'll be the school holidays he thinks and there'll be the children as well. He looks forward to them in particular, as much as he's looking forward to being a grandfather one day, though neither of his daughters have shown any inclination that way so far, despite John's none too subtle hints.

They come into his shop, the young ones especially, their eyes popping as they gaze at the bright, shiny wondrous collections in front of them. Sometimes he tells them little stories about the creatures for whom the shells were once home and they listen in awe and, at their ages, believe.

Some buy his bags of mixed shells, others show him what they've found on the beach, innocent in their need to show him their prized possession. John has been known to give the odd shell away here and there too, if Anne's not looking.

Somewhat reluctantly, Bob Braintree too closes his shop and, with heavy tread, he and Blackwood head for home, this time the cat perched precariously on his shoulder. They keep a close companionship these two, for their mutual benefit and comfort; they can both sense a storm ahead. It's not that either of them is psychic, it's just the norm in their house.

Betty left an hour or so earlier, ostensibly to prepare dinner and finish any domestic chores that remain outstanding. In truth, of course, it affords the both of them the opportunity of a respite from the other's company. The aggravation will surface soon enough as the evening progresses. It's inevitable. Their only hope is that there may be a programme on television able to entertain and interest the both of them, just long enough to keep a semblance of calm in their otherwise troubled world, until bedtime.

This evening, though, the situation is set to deteriorate more rapidly than normal and begins soon after the two companions return home. It's very much a case of, 'she says, he says', or is it the other way around. Either way, the start point is academic and soon lost as the argument intensifies.

It doesn't help the situation when Blackwood decides to join the fray and ensures it turns fully into farce for, though Blackwood may be small, he's agile and cunning. One of his greatest pleasures is terrorising Betty at any given opportunity and this evening he's sensing said opportunity.

Blackwood's technique is simple; he merely has to look intently at Betty's ankles. From experience Betty knows that once she takes her eyes from the cat, even for a second, he'll strike, sinking his teeth and claws into her tender flesh and bone. It's the main reason she's currently backing around the room, desperate to keep distance between them, but as she moves so does Blackwood, keeping the space ever even.

"Keep that cat of yours away from me. He's vicious."

"He's only a little cat," smirks Bob. "He's harmless."

"Harmless! he's evil I tell you. Evil. Like you. They say pets take after their owners and this one certainly does. Shoo! Getaway. Go," and she wafts a tea towel ineffectually in Blackwood's direction. The cat just stalks, savouring the moment, as is Bob.

By now, Betty's been backed to the dresser, the cat poised. Betty, in her anger and frustration, snatches at a plate and smashes it to the floor between them, forcing Blackwood to back-off somewhat and gaining, at the same time, a degree of ascendency, much to Bob's chagrin.

"Why stop at one," Bob says, in raised tones. "Why not smash the bloody lot while you're about it, woman."

"Don't you 'woman' me," and Betty dashes the remaining five to destruction in one fell swoop, shrapnel flying with amazing velocity in all directions.

Blackwood, albeit without benefit of a formal education, instinctively understands the concept of 'discretion being the better part of valour' and hastens to sanctuary underneath the nearest chair. From the safety of distance and with his ears pinned back, the cat hisses his support for Bob whilst directing his venom at Betty.

The last plate shattered does, if nothing else, provides a hiatus in the proceedings as each seeks to draw breath though a certain tension still hangs which is only broken at last by the smell of burning, and the sight of smoke pouring from the oven.

"Bugger," is Bob's only comment as, by mutual, though unspoken consent, the pause button is hit on their current conflagration.

Betty makes no comment as the oven is switched to 'off' and the two of them silently start to clear the mess. Blackwood, however, decides to stay where he is for the time being. Experience tells him that, although things seem calm for the moment, they could flair again at any point.

∞

As some establishments are closing for the evening a few others are beginning to open, anywhere between six and seven o'clock. For them, the restaurants, this is their time of day. Some may have traded a little earlier, offering lunches and afternoon teas, but it's the evening trade that's their highlight, the time when the most of their money's to be made.

This is when the more expensive dishes, the lobsters, crabs, and steaks are bought and eaten, food that's so much healthier for the restauranteurs, certainly their bank accounts, if not the diners themselves.

The Captain, in particular, is already at his station. He's always there at six o'clock, spot on. The door's thrown wide to invite and welcome those for whom a family-friendly menu is more relevant at this hour. It never hurts to earn that little extra, he feels, especially as he'll need to be in station anyway, preparing sauces and trimmings for his more serious of diners still to come.

Out on the promontory Rockabilly's sitting on his terrace, his long legs stretched out before him, glass in hand, facing the sun as it prepares for its slow descent into the west. To his mind, this is the perfect end to a summer's day and far too warm an evening for him to be sitting indoors. Gazing out across the waters, he barely notices the boats, lost as he is to his own thoughts. Alone though not lonely.

For once, he might even cook himself a bite of dinner tonight. He bought some 'bits', as he refers to the bag of food that's now reclining on his kitchen table, in the village earlier, as a precaution. It was a wise decision as it turns out for Rockabilly's feeling far too lazy to walk into Treddoch tonight. He's far too contented where he is.

No, he'll cook he's decided but later though, not just now. After that, he'll strum his guitar most likely, out there, in the open, a surprise to anyone passing on the cliff high path this evening, as the music drifts over them and out across the sea to where he's sure his dream lies waiting.

∞

Lizzy's Mother arrives prompt at six, complete with knitting and a book, ready to bathe and scrub, settle the Little People with a bedtime story whilst Lizzy heads for her evening job, waitressing. The money will be useful, the tips even more so and Lizzy knows how to get the best of tips out of the customers with a smile here, a wink there. It doesn't hurt to be friendly.

It's amazing just how much two Little People can consume, Lizzy often reflects but they're worth it, at least in Lizzy's eyes. At the thought of them, Lizzy will beam a beam that only a mother can and any self-respecting child will shrink from, embarrassed least its peers should see.

Lizzy's Mother's a woman of a quiet demeanour, evenly spoken, a woman with a calm disposition. She's that rare sort of person who's always happy to help anyone, someone who makes time for everyone, regardless of race or creed, wherever and whenever, without thought of recompense in any of its forms.

Lizzy's Mother's a 'good Christian soul' in the broadest sense of the phrase, though she barely sets foot in either Church or Chapel, baptisms, weddings, and funerals the norm and the exception. She's never grasped the connection between being seen devout on Sunday, appropriately dressed in a set of clothes specially reserved for the occasion and, well, not so devout the rest of the week when an uncharitable spirit can often rise to the fore. She remembers Butcher Trelawney's wife.

Yet, for all her goodness of spirit, it seems that Fortune has not reciprocated in kind for Lizzy's Mother's one of those for whom life has never been easy, tinged as it's always been with disappointment and worry. Her day-to-day existence seems to have been a constant struggle. Life's scales have, somehow, always been weighed against her. Fate, it seems, relishes in giving her that gentle kick periodically, a reminder of its ever presence. Uncomplaining though, Lizzy's Mother just burrows on, baring all with an unbending fortitude, her eyes showing evidence of that steely strength that has always carried her through.

Lizzy's Father, a hard-working man, not once a day's sickness in his life until now, has never earned big money and with his recent invalidity earns even less. So, late in life, Lizzy's Mother has had to find a job again, this time in the local Care Home. It's not so much 'to make ends meet' but rather, more to stop the gap widening even further.

Lizzy's Mother has always brought her daughter up to know good from evil, right from wrong, as she holds it so who can know what she must think of Lizzy, husbandless, two offspring and each by a separate father, neither of whom Lizzy lives with, nor wants to either.

Whatever she thinks or feels, Lizzy's Mother keeps a cautious tongue, asking little and is told even less. She does what she can to help.

Abi finishes her part-time job in the General Store at half-past five and heads for home. Some nights it's a case of grabbing at a bite of food before changing clothes, then turning around and moving on to the Fishing Loft where she works as part-time barmaid, mainly, it sometimes seems to her, for Johnny to be able to spend her earnings in The Schooner Inn.

Abi enters the flat, sits back in a chair, kicking off her shoes, grateful that tonight's a night off for she's tired of working, tired of her husband, tired of everything, tired to the point of exhaustion. She just wants to curl up and forget it all. She's reached the limit of her endurance and there's still no sign of the wanderer; he could be anywhere. He's probably back in the pub, Abi suspects, though it's early, even by Johnny's standards.

Through closed and weary eyes Abi sees the banner announcing Armageddon. 'The end is nigh', it's telling her and it is for them. Their personal apocalypse is on the horizon. She remembers a past that had spoken of love, of life, of happiness, of futures and of rings. So far, only the rings have come to pass and she's beginning to feel it's time for their un-forging. She intends telling him tonight, when he comes home. Johnny's on a one-way ticket and it's a trip that's outward bound.

"No more, Johnny, no more. I've had enough," she says, speaking softly, to herself and to the room at large, for there's no one else to speak to. This is where her dream is ending, has ended, for it's a dream no more. It hasn't been for a long time though she can't remember when it transformed into the nightmare that it now is.

"It's over, Johnny, over," and she sobs for herself, for her desperation but mostly for never having realised all, even any, of the dreams she'd once had. They've all gone, the way of all flesh.

Her tears fall as the rains, her hands, in her lap, cling to each other in their desperation.

∞

Unbeknown to Abi, Johnny had returned from his task earlier, exuberant, just as the afternoon was on the wane and made himself another cheese sandwich which this time he ate with extra relish.

He was on top form, all of a sudden, burning with a feverish heat, though this time not from the after-effects of alcohol. He couldn't wait to tell Abi but equally he couldn't wait for Abi. He had so much to do, so much to do. The inspiration and the willingness were on him, akin to the laying on of hands.

He was much like the White Rabbit, in his frantic hurry. "Can't wait, can't wait." There was so much lost time in need of recapture, so many things to say to Abi, but that part could wait, till the evening. For the now, for once, Johnny was a man with a mission.

It's certainly wasn't that Johnny didn't want to see Abi. On the contrary, he did; desperately. In particular, he'd wanted to explain to her where he'd been and, more importantly now, where he's going, where they're both going but the fever was on him and taken hold. He couldn't wait, just couldn't.

Refreshed in both body and soul Johnny had flown to the cliffs, sketchbook and pencils in hand.

As the sobbing subsides, first to a sniffle, then to a stop, Abi brings herself together, heading first to the bathroom to wash her face, then into the bedroom to change her clothes. Seeing the pictures on the bed they remind her that she needs to tidy them away. She's forgotten she'd left them there this morning.

Abi starts to gather them together, pulling them into a pile so she can roll them and return them to the dark recess of her wardrobe where she feels they best belong. It's only as she's herding them that she notices the very recent addition, the portrait of a cat.

It's Bastet for certain. Yes, most definitely, Bastet, pure and simple. Well no, not simple. It's definitely Bastet, but not simple, for Abi's attention's immediately drawn to the eyes which seem to burn the very fabric on which they've been embossed.

It's a good portrait of Bastet, very good. Abi would even go so far as to say, exceptional and considering the feelings Abi's holding towards Johnny that's more than generous.

Johnny has caught The Cat well in general, but it's the eyes that captivate. Even in paint, they pull the viewer in. They're totally hypnotic.

Abi weeps again, though this time with tears of joy. She isn't sure what's happened; what's happening but something has, is, she knows. Johnny's painting again. Surely, it can only be for the good, can't it? The portrait, is it a portent of things to come she can only wonder? She hopes so. Abi has to hope. There's little other choice for it seems that's all she has left, Hope, and even that's been left teetering on the brink this last while.

Mopping her eyes again, Abi heads to the kitchen to make a cup of tea, but, on impulse, opens the refrigerator door instead, remembering there's half a bottle of wine, lurking.

She turns to reach for a glass from the cupboard. It's then that she notices Johnny's old painting box, the one that's lain dead in the shed for so long, there, in the corner, open. Its contents are a shambles. Clearly, something's afoot but whatever it is, seeing the mess in the corner clearly not quite everything's changed with Johnny. The mess, though, she can live with.

Abi smiles as she sips. Her first smile in a very long time. Suddenly the missing years begin to roll away. It's been a long time, but it seems it may have been worth the wait after all.

It's back to the bathroom, wine glass firmly grasped in hand and another wash. Then, into the bedroom for fresh clothes and perfume, something she hasn't bothered with for a long time. Until now, there'd seemed little point.

Looking at the portraits of herself she restyles her hair, with the ponytail, and applies some make-up. Like the perfume, she adds a little more than has been usual of late and, finally, she hunts through the contents of her handbag. It's still there, after all this time, the pink lipstick.

Dressed and with make-up on Abi checks herself in the mirror as she takes another sip. The ponytail, the pink lipstick are as they once were. Looking down the front of her jumper though, her breasts no longer seem quite as perky as her portrait suggests. O, well, they'll have to take their chances she thinks. Can't have everything. Two out of three and all that.

And Abi sips as she sits and waits.

Old Bill is a creature of set routine and order. After lunch, with the Nancarrow sisters, he goes home and waits quietly, as far as anyone knows, though no one's quite sure until the village clock strikes six.

On the stroke of six, very precisely, Bill leaves his small flat, door never locked, and heads for the Fishing Loft, via the Church, not for any reason of confessional but to play the organ. Quite unbelievably, Bill is the Church Organist in Treddoch Harbour, hence a key, clutched proudly in his right hand giving him unfettered access to Church premises.

Bill's was a lonely childhood, pretty much shunned as he was by his peers. Children can be quite heartless, and they were. No one really wanted to play with him; they made it very clear.

Whereas it might have upset others it never seemed to have bothered Bill. He certainly never showed any signs that it might have but then, what went on inside Bill's head was known only to Bill and whatever god he has.

Though slow of brain in general academic matters and with no athletic ability whatsoever, Bill has an affinity with music. It's a gift, some say, from God himself as recompense.

No one seems to know for certain, the exact sequence of events that led to Bill's love affair with music in general and the Church organ in particular. The best that can be traced seems to lie in the fact that every Sunday, from an infant, Bill would attend Church, the large, medieval one in St. Wyllow, with his mother, who would thank the Lord, sincerely, for her daily bread and The Baker who provided it, single woman, as she was.

With, perhaps, little else filling the poor lad's head, The Music of the organ may well have found a void to occupy. Realising that its host actually welcomed the insurgent, it stayed, and multiplied, taking over, consuming all within, till the two, Bill and the music, were one. Speculation at best, but St. Wyllow's an even smaller place than Treddoch Harbour.

What is fact though, is that Bill was about ten when he startled The Organist of the time. He was one of the Penprase family, big churchgoers for generations, (you can read their history in the church graveyard) by suddenly appearing slightly behind and to the right of his shoulder when the Organist was at practice. Absorbed in his playing, the organist hadn't heard Bill's near-silent approach over the sound of the notes and Bill wasn't one to push himself forward. Shunned by his peers Bill had already learned to keep his profile low.

Momentarily startled, The Organist hit a bad note which made even Bill, untutored though he was at the time, wince but both soon recovered their composures.

"Hello Boy; sorry, but you startled me. Didn't see you standing there. Have you been here long?"

Bill nodded dumbly.

"Do you like music?"

Another nod.

"Do you play?" though The Organist didn't think so. Given the minuscule size of the hamlet there's very little there, if anything, that's a total secret.

This time, a shake of the head to suggest a negative.

Undeterred, The Organist persisted. He had children of his own, though now long grown. He still remembered the need for patience on occasion and fortunately for Bill, The Organist was a patient man by nature.

"Would you like to learn?"

This time a very vigorous shake of the head and an almost smile. The Organist took this as a positive and that was the diaried beginning to Bill's musical advancement.

The Organist took Bill under his wing and taught him as much as he knew himself but soon realised that Bill was something of a protégée with his playing.

In different circumstances something might have been done to promote this ability but in Bill's case he was left to enjoy himself without stress or pressure, neither of which he'd probably have managed with. Bill was content in his playing and they let the lad be with that. It was generally considered good that Bill had found some niche in life.

Later in life, when he was given a place to work and then, a place to live, in Treddoch, he eventually gravitated to the role of Organist here. It's been considered a great loss to the hamlet whose inhabitants still often request his guest appearance when their own and newer incumbent isn't available.

Bill took to the organ as a fledgling to the skies except that the notes that flow through Bills fingers soar out of the organ pipes and rise way beyond the reach of gulls and gannets until, some are wont to say, they reach the very threshold of Heaven itself. It's even been asserted that the angels lower their harps to listen.

That's a touch of hyperbole for certain but, maybe, Bill's musical talent is indeed a gift from God; who knows? It might well seem to be an amendment for Bill's other shortcomings, a compensation. If that's so then Bill certainly repays Him in kind.

Come Sunday Bill plays for the declining congregation, helping them lift their joyful voices, but, of an evening, during the rest of the week, Bill plays for his personal pleasure.

As tourists, should you venture off the road a little, by way of the Church, you'll be sure to hear Bill's music seeping through granite thick walls, flowing out into the ether. Pause a moment to listen, I'm sure you'll be pleased.

Johnny and Abi's tracks must have missed earlier in their crossing by little more than a hair's breadth as they each moved their separate ways. Johnny's journey to the cliffs was hurried and with purpose, eager to progress, Abi's was a heavier tread towards home; slow and deliberate.

She was thoughtful; pondering the inevitable argument with Johnny that she was sure was forthcoming. For Abi, this seemed to be another defining moment in her life, not, in its way, dissimilar to the one where she'd said, "Yes," to Johnny's proposal.

At the same moment that Abi was approaching their flat,

Johnny had settled himself on a back-side numbing lump of rock. It was the price to be paid, he reflected; due punishment. It also afforded a perfect view of the sea to both east and west and, glancing down, the harbour as well, the latter now water filled with the rising tide.

All about, to left, to right and to below, boats abound on this calm of a summer's evening, boats of all varieties, all sizes, all colours, boats of both sail and engine. In all, they're a veritable gift to any artist but especially to one with such an urgent need to recover time already frittered.

After quick deliberation, Johnny decides to settle his attention on the harbour first. These are the pictures that always sell best, easy reference points as they are to visitors, reminders, when back wherever they've come from, of happy hours spent in idealistic places all too soon so far away.

He thinks it must be Tom he can see, standing, watching the waters and without yet realising the poignancy of his decision Johnny feels he must most definitely include Tom in his drawings if only for that touch of authenticity.

Johnny sketches, fast and furious; his pencil skitting across page after page as he records outlines to be fleshed out later. No time for fill now. He's hungry for ideas, eager to capture moments, desperate to recover lost time.

The Trendy Young Couple passing close by on their cliff walk, are momentarily taken aback to see Johnny so ardent in his work and not in the pub. He's about to call out but She puts a hand on his arm.

"Leave him be," she says. "Looks like he might actually be working for once," and they chuckle together as they move on, unnoticed by Johnny, absorbed as he is in the pages of his sketchbook. For the moment, as he's sketching, nothing else exists, not even Abi.

# Last Thing

Summer's solstice is drawing to conclusion. Midsummer is close to closing for another year as evening begins to settle in layers, like a fine dust, on the little village.

The sun, for all its summer-seeming permanence, is sliding doggedly into the west, signalling the end of a long, long day. A few straggling strands of light linger in their final, albeit vain, attempt to stave off the black that's as inevitable as will be a fresh, new beginning, tomorrow.

From this point on, village days can only shorten. Imperceptibly though it may seem at the beginning, time will drive relentlessly on towards yet another Autumn, another Winter. Circles know neither beginning nor end; they merely go around, as pre-defined.

For the villagers though, at this moment, Autumn, let alone Winter is still a long way off, and nowhere in their sights. For the moment it's Summer; a time for cheer. The Season is all but full upon them. There's still the hope of money to be made; dreams to be fulfilled.

"If only, if only, if only," they silently plead, "the sun will shine for just a couple of months and the rains go somewhere else. Anywhere but here."

"Please Lord, let's not have a wet Summer," is added to the communal prayer, the communal dream.

Outside of the pubs all starts to fall quiet. The day visitors have long gone and most of the locals have retreated to their homes. One way and another, the villagers settle for the evening, preparing for sleep, ready to recharge for the morrow, ready to re-visit their own, their personal dreams.

Dreams of purchases yet to be made, dreams of far-away holidays in exotic seas, dreams of wedding rings and of babies yet to be, once the money's in. All are dreams until made real as some most definitely will and others most definitely won't.

∞

The visitors too will have their dreams tonight, as assorted as the shells on Treddoch beach. For a few, they will be dreams of Treddoch itself, dreams of living here in this seeming idyll, so remote, as it is, from their urban existence.

For the occasional one their dream will come true, at some point. It can only be hoped it meets with their expectations.

∞

On top of the hill, deep in the dark, dank loam that is the cemetery, twilight holds as little meaning as does the succeeding dawn. Here, night is guaranteed, as perpetual as is death itself.

For The Butcher and his Wife, their one conversation will remain interminable, looped for the length of eternity. It will be the same conversation as it was when you were introduced to them this morning, as it will be tomorrow morning, as it will be every day.

It wasn't always like it is now though, for The Butcher and his Wife. Once upon a time, and not so very long ago, they would have lain side by side as they are now, though fully winceyetted as they were then. The Butcher's Wife would have turned towards Butcher Trelawney and said, "Goodnight, Butcher, see you in the morning."

In turn, the Butcher would have replied, "Goodnight, Mrs. Trelawney. In the morning. Sleep well." They would have kissed lightly and then rolled over, back to back, (theirs had never been a relationship based on a passion of great proportions), she, thinking of rings still to be bought, he, thinking of carcasses in need of being ordered.

Now they lie together as bare of flesh as they are of winceyette. Forever. No more 'Goodnights, sleep wells', no more mornings, no more dreams of time to come, though even in death the Butcher's Wife will still remember her once gold rings long since lost and The Butcher, his long-lamented slaughterhouse.

∞

The Captain's Table has closed for the night. Port and starboard lights are lit on either side of the building. The Captain has retired to his inner sanctum for a few minutes of peace, sole male as he is in a house of female kind, and is having his nightly tot of rum, drawn from his ship's decanter.

Rum, like the whiskers, and the rolling gait are all part of an appearance that the years and the sea-faring role have cultivated. They attire him like his Guernsey sweater and his cap.

The Captain, of course, will dream of seas past sailed, though bluer now, filtered as they will be, through the medium of sleep, of time and of distance.

∞

As The Captain's drinking his contented rum so Jack is sitting with a crystal of golden malt. He swirls it absentmindedly, sipping a little here, a little there, bringing a comfort to both body and soul, though it's long distant from being a cold evening. If anything, weather-wise, it's the complete reverse, but this is the point of the day, that rare occasion, when life loses its normal bleakness for Jack, if only for a briefest of moments and is replaced with a tinge of colour, even if it's whisky gold.

The only other occasion Jack's spirits lift is, as we've witnessed, when Lizzy breezes into his shop of a morning. Well, not his shop exactly, as everyone is now well aware and Tamsyn is wont to continually remind him.

Like all the other trappings, Jack often feels he's just another item on Tamsyn's asset sheet to be mentally 'ticked off' when she undertakes one of her audits, which she does, with an increasing frequency.

Jack's has become a marriage as barren of love as it is, fortunately he tends to think, of children. Fortunate, for there'll be less pain in the parting when it comes as surely it must. One day, it will happen, and that day is drawing ever nearer he feels.

With every passing hour, particularly since the death of her parents and receiving her inheritance, *her inheritance*, Tamsyn is growing as mean of spirit as she is of purse. In his quieter moments, Jack often wonders, as he is doing now, how he fell into it. Like his late mother-in-law, he sold himself for little more than a roof over his head, fire in a winter's hearth and a rib of beef on Sunday. At least the Butcher's Wife also had her gold rings. If nothing else, they were some sort of consolation prize.

In his whiskied thoughts, Jack thinks of Lizzy. Bright, bouncing Lizzy, 'Fizzy Lizzy', Lizzy with the warm and lively smile and wide, clear eyes. Lizzy with the bronzed thighs and joyful greeting of a morning which for even those few, precious moments, lifts Jack's spirits.

Jack looks forward to Lizzy's morning visits and is already anticipating tomorrow's, though with perhaps just a touch more enthusiasm than his married status might warrant. He ignores his conscience for now; the whisky helps.

On the spur, he decides to ensure that he gives her a little extra weight in her purchase tomorrow, and not charge for it. It's an heretical thought, he knows and one that should have Butcher Trelawney revolving in his grave!

Jack chuckles a wicked chuckle and raises his glass to the thought. "Saluté."

Tamsyn, confused by his action, looks across from where she's sitting, counting the day's take – for the second time. Jack's disturbed her rhythm; she'll have to start over again.

Perhaps when he falls asleep tonight Jack will dream of olive eyes, short skirts, bronzed thighs; things all designed to confuse and confound him and make him squirm, all the more, when he sees Lizzy again on a more sober tomorrow.

It'll be a long time before Tamsyn falls asleep tonight, as with every night. Tamsyn doesn't sleep well these days. Her money worries her especially the thought of losing any of it. It's burden, though, is a blessing too and Tamsyn will mentally run through her asset list in the quiet hours, probably several times, just to be sure nothing's escaped when she wasn't looking.

She's clearly overlooked Jack.

Lizzy has returned from work, kissed her mother on the cheek and thanked her, as she does every night, for her babysitting duties. Come the end of The Season Lizzy will be sure to treat her to a little something, something special, something she wouldn't normally buy for herself. Her mother rarely has funds for any of life's indulgences.

In the meantime, she counts her tips, puts them in a tin marked 'Biscuits' (at the same time the evicted biscuits are being illogically conserved in a plastic lidded tub) and enters the amount in the back of her diary.

Unlike Tamsyn though, Lizzy is in no ways mean, either in spirit or in manner. She's just careful. She has to be for Lizzy and The Little People will need that cash in the winter days ahead to make sure there're plenty of little treats as well as necessities. Little treats for Little People Lizzy thinks, chuckles at her own whimsy and smiles, with a satisfied look upwards to their room above.

Her happiness is only doused a little as she thinks of poor Uncle Tom, nightly alone in his old male world, with no one to care for him and, equally, no one to care for.

Generally, Lizzy's dreams are varied and uncomplicated, but that may be about to change, the uncomplicated aspect that is. Tonight, Lizzy's likely to find images of Jack starting to slip surreptitiously in amongst them which will leave her surprised and startled come the morning. She might even blush when she sees Jack, which she's sure to.

There's no way Lizzy will miss a trip to Jack's.

The Nancarrow sisters sit, as always, side by side in their now unfashionably upholstered but impeccably clean chairs, chirruping away as always. Although early risers, they stay up quite late, catching up on any wanted sleep by way of an afternoon snooze, both at the same time of course, after the Bakery's closed.

They chirp and chatter about many things across the course of the evening but little is ever said by either, though they both think worried thoughts, in unison, as to what will become of the village if there's no Bakery and, worst of all, a Bakery not run by a Nancarrow.

For the both of them, this is a dream too dire to contemplate; one to be put aside for another day.

∞

Old Bill is undoubtedly in his flat, though no one knows exactly of what his evenings comprise once he's left the pub.

He does have a television and it's always been assumed that he sits and watches that, though no one can ever recall him commenting on any programme to date, but then Bill's never been one to engage in active conversation anyway. In fact, it's quite the reverse with Bill; he's always kept his peace. Bill is an introverted soul.

As no one really knows the exactness of his movements, for once, in village life, no one tries to second-guess. He always seems content and, as long as he is, then the villagers are too.

Bill's is an uncomplicated mind, as straightforward as his life, composed as it is of attending The Bakery and playing the organ. It's can only be assumed that any dreams he may have will centre on either of these. But who knows? Dreams, as a subject, are something Bill would never think to discuss.

∞

The Braintree house is quiet for now and has been for much of the evening following the plate smashing episode of earlier. Dinner was a bit of a problem, given that their chosen meat was burned to crisp and it was too late for emergency fish and chips from The Saucy Cod.

Fortunately, there were bits in the freezer from which, working silently together, they were able to concoct a passing semblance to a meal which was eaten off plates freshly acquired from their shop.

Blackwood's tea was in a sealed tin, so he was exempt from the disaster and is now contentedly sitting on the patio outside, washing his paws, thinking of visiting his lady friend, two doors down, whilst his owners continue their silence in front of the television.

When they go to bed tonight, as they sink towards sleep, they will both think dark and venomous thoughts as they always do, always have done; thoughts as to how the other one might die and what, in their imaginings, they can each do to help hasten the process.

Bob will think of suitable accidents that might befall Betty and Betty, for her part, will think of what unpleasant poisons she could administer to Bob; poisons that would be as painful as they are effective.

Neither of them thinks past that point, certainly not to the time when, almost inevitably, one will pre-decease the other. How long will the surviving one remain themselves then, with no one to focus their bile on?

Dinner eaten, crockery washed and tidied away, school books marked for the evening, Molly sits in her chair, spoon-backed and deep buttoned, a book on her lap, a glass of wine, chilled, and two chocolates on the table to her side. Alone and lonely. There's not even The Cat for company on such a summer's night as this.

"Out hunting," suspects Molly, as she turns another page. "She'll come in when she wants, certainly when she wants feeding." Molly likes to think she knows Bastet.

Molly is a great reader. Much as she might love Treddoch Harbour, land of her birth, place of her work, books give Molly that freedom to roam an ever-expanding globe and all that's contained therein.

She views reading as part of an endless journey where, with every page she turns she learns something new, expanding the personal depths of her knowledge. It will be only when Molly goes to sleep tonight and dreams her eternal dream that Molly will realise, as she always does, that even books are no substitute for what she really wants. Some things, like love, have to be lived and felt in the real world; they can't be obtained second hand.

You may think you know of what Molly will dream tonight but be prepared. In part, you'll be correct, but Molly's dreams have heightened with time. Desires and expectations have been elevated. The bar has been steadily raised and all the result of too much reading, an increasingly vivid imagining and not enough living, the villagers would say if Molly dared divulge which, of course, she daren't.

Molly's mind has become a cauldron where, like the county in which she so delights, fact and fiction can so easily become entwined.

Molly still dreams her dreams of a husband to be but now, her dreams are no longer any old dreams, nor are they dreams of any old husband.

Molly now dreams of Camelot, of Arthur and his knights, of being whisked away on a black charger, a charger the colour of midnight, its gold bridle more brilliant than the sun which would dare compete with it.

She dreams of Launcelot on this midnight steed, Launcelot, tall, dark and dashing, to whom she throws her favour to garland his lance, as he rescues her from the imprisonment of spinsterhood.

Molly's dreams have grown more exotic and erotic as the years have passed, her expectations of a rescuer now lifted to mythical extent. As counterbalance Molly's chances of fulfilment wane proportionately. Soon, they'll pass into legend, as Camelot has.

Louise, who never dreamed of having another man in her life after Bertie now has one. Regardless of age, she's as giddy as a schoolgirl as she counts just how many more sleeps there are to be before Robert returns. Too many, it seems, though she only has to wait till the end of the week. It will soon come, though not soon enough to Louise's mind.

In readiness, she's been on a shopping trip to the city and overhauled her collection of lingerie. The scantiest of nighties is hanging, expectantly, in her wardrobe.

Joan and Henry sit smug and superior in their understated, yet exquisitely decorated conservatory, with carefully selected plants and strategically placed magazines arranged on the coffee table for maximum effect. There's not a crease in sight whether it be magazine, plant or table.

This, at least, is how Joan sits as she works hard to disremember her past. The particulars are certainly diminishing with the passing of days and the building of a new existence, but the aura of cold and hunger still haunts her quieter moments. She's working hard to eradicate that as well.

Henry's a little less comfortable with his new life than Joan, though not his chair. He can't fault Joan's taste in interior design.

They watch the sun set over a silk-smooth Channel and sip a cocktail as they have done for the past few nights. Normally, each would have a glass of wine in their hands; a red for Henry, a chilled white for Joan. All very civilised and almost elegant to Joan's way of thinking.

Things, however, have changed of late as Joan looks to elevate herself yet a touch further. Since having cornered Henry, Joan's been on a roller-coaster that, so far, has only ever gained in height.

Her social snobbery remains boundless and unfettered. She's recently read, in one of her more upmarket glossies, just how trendy cocktails are becoming with the 'in-crowd' and Joan has definitely always wanted to be 'in'. Still being able to recall being 'out' only serves to reinforce her determination not only to be 'in' but super-glued there to boot.

On a recent visit to the town, Joan had discovered by chance and coincidence, in a Charity Shop (not that she'd ever admit to entering one), a book on the very subject of cocktails.

Fortified in the knowledge that life, in recent years, has definitely been moving her in the right direction and is continuing to do so, Joan had headed back to her eyrie on the clifftop. There, she presented her find, as a cat might a dead bird to its owner, to an amazed Henry who could only continue to wonder where Fate was continuing to push him.

Sitting, drink in hand, glazed eyes looking out over a languid sea, too leaden, this warm, solstice night, to barely raise a ripple to ruffle its surface, Henry wonders why he'd left his wife of so many years.

If nothing else, it had been a comfortable existence, like wearing an old jumper, (something he's not allowed to do now), without a need for dinner parties, drinks parties or any other parties. He also had his children as well in those days. They've gone the way of cards on Father's Day and fast becoming a dimming memory.

He would like to say that he holds the hand life's dealt him but he knows full well, in an honest moment, that it's he himself if not having actually dealt it, has fully, openly and unquestioningly, accepted it.

Life now is what it is. It's best not to think about it too much, just get on with it; be resigned to the fact. He knows, for certain, that there's no going back.

Joan, is also mindful of their differing ages. She's not yet old, on any definition. Indeed, she's maturing very attractively, with no need to attend to the roots of her hair, holding, as they still do, their natural colour. The highlights are put in purely for style and fashion. Joan likes to highlight as many aspects of her life as possible.

As need demands, Joan visits her hairdresser in the city; nearer ones are far too parochial for her tastes. It's something which occasions comment, when not in-ear, from other females of her fraternity, who, in general perhaps, pay less attention to their appearance than Joan does.

The males of their group tend to be the more impressed and regard Henry as a 'lucky old dog'. Some would be more than happy to trade places on the chance, without first undertaking any due diligence. Lack of due diligence was Henry's mistake he's sometime wont to think.

Looking across at Henry, Joan can see early signs of grey seeping into the edges of his hair. Not much, but the beginnings all the same. They'll need attention before they announce themselves to all and sundry.

Joan makes a mental note to do something about that tomorrow, at the same time bringing to the fore the concept of a wedding which, as yet, is a subject she hasn't broached. After all, a girl needs to think of her future.

Neither Joan nor Henry are particularly ecstatic over any of the cocktail concoctions that Henry's so far made, far from it, but, to his horror and dismay, Joan has insisted they persevere. She's confident 'he'll do better' with practice. It's still a new experience and, with a little positive perseverance, one they can share with their friends when they throw their next dinner party.

"O ye gods!" thinks Henry, wishing for his glass of wine, or, better still, a bottle of beer, as he once had, when married which is why, when he sleeps tonight, Henry will dream of nothing; his mind will be a blank. He's trained it that way.

Henry's long learned that dreaming can be bad for his health; wanting, positively hazardous. He believes that dreams should come with a health warning and in plain wrapping. It's best not to dream any more he feels, just get on with gritty reality and accept what he has, for good or for ill.

Joan will dream of dignified and beautiful futures as per habit, but glimpses of the past have a habit of sneaking in amongst them. She's never been able to fully delete them so far, try as she might, and Joan has certainly tried.

A bottle of beer is exactly what Jason Henley's enjoying as he sits, slippered comfortable, side by side with Sarah in front of their television. It's been a good day in the shop with takings now on a rising trend as The Season's progressing. All-in-all, Jason can't see much wrong with life, tonight or at any other time really.

As a bonus to life's bounties for Jason, most Sundays, weather permitting and outside of Season when seven-day working is a must, out comes his trusty old camper van to trundle them all to a picnic somewhere on the Moor.

The difference these days though, is that it's now a trusty old camper and not a rusty one anymore. That battered rust-bucket of his youth has now been fully restored and has morphed into a very collectable classic of certain value. He drives it with more care these days too, though he stills calls it Nellie, as he always did.

Nellie was his Grandmother's name. The name originally given with the irreverence of adolescence is now retained with a touch of tender reflection for a lady for whom Jason holds particularly fond memories.

The only other reminder of his long distant arrival in Treddoch and a nod to his disappearing youth is his old earring which still sits as confident in his ear as a parrot might on his shoulder with the added benefit that the earring neither talks nor poops down his back.

As he sits musing, Jason's old dream stops by for a quick visit, much like an old friend, whom he hasn't seen for some time, dropping in for a chat.

"It's been a long while, Jason. Do you ever think of me these days?"

"Very rarely, only when I've nothing better to do, which isn't often, given my life now, full as it is."

He half turns to his wife and smiles, just at the sight of her, leaving his dream, feeling no longer wanted, to see itself out.

His wife, as comfortable as a cat on a gossamer cushion, returns an almond-eyed smile, snuggling a little closer. She'd purr if she could.

Jason has already dealt with his dream for this night and given it short shrift; Jason is Sarah's dream and always has been.

Allan and Jenifer sit, relaxed, much like Jason and Sarah. They have similar relationships. Both couples, have relatively uncomplicated lives.

Jenifer isn't usually troubled in sleep, certainly not recently. Previously, there was a period when she worried that Young Kenver was turning into his grandfather, William. The thought kept her awake at nights. But that has now moved to the past.

Tonight, such thoughts will be far away as is Young Kenver at this very moment, in far-flung Singapore. Life, for Kenver, has changed course in recent time, somewhat dramatically and for the better. It seems he may be at the start of making his own way in the world. It's certainly eased his mother's concerns and sweetened her dreams.

Allan will sleep deep and sound. Little disturbs him. The only thing to worry Allan is Jenifer herself being worried. She's his primary concern. Now that Kenver's future no longer disturbs her, Allan is no longer disturbed himself.

If Allan should dream it will be of something so trivial and inconsequential that he won't remember it come morning; his cup of tea will be foremost in his mind at that time.

∞

When Rose settles down tonight her thoughts will turn to Rockabilly, not the steady, reliable, husband lying beside her, exhausted from working hard, to earn the money, to pay the bills Rose so disdains.

Rose still cherishes that lunchtime kiss, however chaste and the hand on her waist. All day, the vision of Rockabilly lying languidly in bed has moved with her and moved her. In her dreams, another kiss, so she hopes, will not be so innocent.

As much as Rose may dream though, come the end, it will only ever be that, a dream.

Rockabilly Joe will probably be the last to retire in Treddoch tonight. He usually is. The last man standing, or rather sitting, as he perches from now to somewhere past midnight on a straight-backed chair, looking out his large, open glass door, out across the sea towards western lands.

He strums his guitar quietly to himself, singing songs he once sang to an audience that would fill a stadium and more recent songs that he writes for just himself and for Her, the woman across the sea.

Tonight there's no audience; there's no one to listen to him. No cat, no dog; not even a mouse. The birds have all settled for the night. Even the West Wind has deserted him, the air's so still. His songs though, are not so much sad, as solitary. They are songs from a man alone, for a girl somewhere else. These are waiting songs.

Tonight, Rockabilly will dream once more of the girl coming to him from over a western sea, ember hair and cloak flying behind her, drawn to his songs. He'll wait for her. He knows she will come, one day, in person. The West Wind will bring her.

∞

John Tregear is sitting with Anne, each enjoying their final cup of tea of the day, Anne contentedly watching television, John, half-reading a book on shells. Unusually, he's finding it difficult to concentrate tonight much as he might try. After every few lines, John's mind slips back to earlier, to Tom and their meeting around the harbour.

They'd met as they always met at that time of night, but Tom most certainly wasn't his usual self. John can't quite reason what was wrong, but something definitely was. Somehow, 'distant', is the only word John can think to describe Tom. Somewhere far away. Very far. Almost otherworldly. There had seemed to be a weariness hanging over him.

Tom hadn't had much to say either, which was unusual for Tom, vociferous as he normally is with his stories and his tales. When he did speak it was as if his voice had grown suddenly old, even just since the morning.

John had tried to draw a conversation from him but it had proved hard work, the effort all one-sided. In the end, John had given in and returned home a little earlier than his normal dead-on-the-dot seven o'clock as prescribed by Anne.

Even Anne was surprised, asking if there was a problem, with John she'd meant, always concerned as she is for his health. John explained but all Anne did was to shrug her shoulders, pointing out Tom's advancing age and the peculiarities that can come with it.

John, ostensibly, and not wishing to spoil their dinner time, accepted Anne's interpretation but privately worried.

"Something's not right," he says to the evening. He can smell an ill wind just as he could once smell the pilchards as they were shoaling.

∞

As with every other solitary night of his empty existence for the past however many years, Tom has had his evening tour of the harbour, though he really wasn't in a mood for conversation this evening. That was something unusual for him which he'd noted. He guessed John had noticed it too; he'd gone in earlier than usual after all. Tom's mind's been far distant, ever since returning from his solicitor. Its connection with his body is growing less and less tangible.

He's said goodnight to the boats now resting, made his peace with the harbour and is now returned to the quiet confines of his ancient cottage, lit, for the moment, with only the incandescent glow of a streetlamp outside his window. It's enough for tonight. Tonight, Tom can see all he wants or needs to see.

Sinking heavy into his hearth-side chair, holding tight to the arms for that extra support, satisfied with the day's events, comforted with the fact that he has said all the goodbyes he ever needs to say, especially to his harbour, Tom slides into that sweet dark where the real and the unreal begin to merge.

Reality begins to slip away as the weight of time no longer hangs as heavy as it once did. His breathing shallows; his thoughts move straight to his long-ago Mary.

"I'll be seeing you soon, old girl," he whispers to the cottage-dark night. "Very soon, I think."

Time ticks on the mantlepiece clock that was once a wedding present.

Slumped back, with but the softest of breath left, enfolded by dreams, seeing only with his mind, Tom sights her, his Mary, once more, across the water, on the far quay, summer frocked and sandaled, hair tied neatly back, all smiles and waving arm. It's the way Tom always sees her, his Mary.

"I'm waiting, Tom, just as I've always waited for you." Silent words drift across the lightly lapping waters, but they're voluble to Tom, nonetheless.

As the clock strikes the hour, and with a fair wind behind him, Tom slips his moorings and sets out on the night tide, charting his final crossing.

Tom has dreamed his last dream; now he's living it. Tom and his Mary, together again. Finally, and for eternity. Tom could have wished for no more.

The only two of the day's players already in bed are Abi and Johnny, she, smiling and content in the crook of his arm; both a first for a long time. Johnny had returned from the cliffs just a little earlier, fortified not with beer this time but with sketches, purpose and a plan, albeit a tentative one at this stage but a plan, nevertheless.

Abi had waited his return patiently, with hope and a rising passion. Half a bottle of wine was helping.

Come eight o'clock the light was passing its best for Johnny's purposes so, in some ways reluctantly, he'd closed his sketchbook, packed his pencils into their case and headed for home and Abi, concerned for the welcome he was expecting.

Passing through the village he'd met with a couple of friends, well, drinking buddies really, from The Schooner Inn.

"Joining us, Johnny?" asked the one, expecting an almost automatic 'yes', so he was surprised to hear a "No thanks. Off home, Abi'll be waiting," as Johnny continued his stride.

The one pal half turned to the other, a questioning look on his face.

"No idea." That, and a shake of the head was the only response, to which the former gave a shrug of his shoulders, dismissing the matter entirely, for the moment, though it was sure to be discussed, and with a wider audience, once the first pints were pulled.

Johnny had entered the flat with a certain amount of trepidation to find Abi, sitting quietly, glass in hand, hair in a ponytail, lips fully pinked, fingernails newly glistening with polish. The television was turned firmly to the 'off' position.

"Well?" she said, but in softer tones, than he could have possibly ever imagined. "I think an explanation's in order, don't you?"

Johnny stood transfixed; a rabbit momentarily caught in headlights. Gathering what wits remained he explained, and explained, and explained, grateful for such a light punishment; the equivalent of community service as opposed to the custodial sentence he'd been expecting.

The early portraits of Abi have been rolled for safekeeping, but not returned to the dark recesses that have for so long enclosed them. They're to be the start of Johnny's portfolio which Johnny is to add to, systematically. He's happily agreed to that.

Bastet's portrait is fixed carefully to the bedroom wall. It's the one picture never to be sold. Johnny's even promised to have it framed tomorrow.

Johnny has also to start work, first thing tomorrow, on this evening's sketches. It's looking to be his busiest day for a long time. Maybe his busiest ever, to date. Cheese and pickle sandwiches will feature heavily on his menu together with cups of tea, lots of cups of tea.

"We will be alright, won't we?" Abi asks uncertainly, the memory of the all-too-recent past loitering there, in the background.

"Of course we will," Johnny says reassuringly. For the first time since he could remember, Johnny sees an evolving future, like a photograph in a developing tray but one without the necessity of beer for a fixative.

Lying there, rethinking old thoughts, feeling renewed hope of life with Johnny, Abi even remembers the name of the cat that has, so far, never been, but, perhaps, soon will.

For Johnny, his artist's eyes have looked inside his father's grave and seen bare bones. That's all the old man was left with, nothing else. A box of bones. That's not to be his future. He's now determined.

"Thank you," he says, kissing her lightly on the forehead.

"For what?"

"For simply being."

A tear slides down a cheek as Abi snuggles even closer, close enough now for him now to feel her heart beating against his chest.

"What's been has been, what's gone has gone, I can never make it right, but I can make it better."

Rose would be envious if she had even a portion of knowledge as to how close these two are lying tonight, comfortable again, as they once were.

∞

As for The Cat, Bastet, she's sitting on the harbour wall, not 'mousing' as her owner suspects. For Bastet, 'mousing' is a sport, not a pursuit of food. The thought of eating cold, raw mouse sends shivers through her regal frame.

A cat, so perfect of poise and paw, Bastet is formed of finer tastes. She prefers her meats cooked, perhaps with a little cereal added though best of all, of course, some freshly steamed fish. Cold, dead mouse. Urgh! An anathema.

Framed against a rising moon, nose high into the night air, drawing in the summer scents that surround her, shoulders taut, back straight, tail curved around, Bastet holds as smug an expression as a cat can muster.

All in all, she feels, it's been a good day, though she does have to question why she'd let the mouse escape. Clearly, she's been living amongst these humans for far too long.

"Could do better," she chastises herself.

Do cats dream? It's possible. If so, of what will Bastet dream tonight, when she finally settles for sleep? To be stretched, languid, under a palm, for shade, sheltering from the blazing sun of a Nile sky?

Perhaps. Who knows?

Best ask The Cat, but don't be too alarmed if you find she tells you. After all, this *is* Treddoch Harbour and this *is* Cornwall. There's still a little magic left.

---

# *About the Author*

Ian was born in the Midlands a long time back and has only taken to writing rather late in life.

He graduated from the University of East Anglia (UEA) with a degree in economics but even in those days harboured literary ambitions. They were just slow in coming to the fore.

After graduation, he worked, briefly, as an Economist in London but soon moved to Cornwall, where, together with his wife, he ran his own business for many years. They lived in the small Cornish fishing village of Polperro which has provided a rich source of material for Ian's first novel, 'Midsummer Dreams'.

Ian began work on the novel in January 2017 and eight months later had a rough draft ready but feeling the need for a break from it put the manuscript to one side and thought to write just a couple of short stories.

Twelve months and fifteen stories later it became clear that Ian had his first volume, 'Collected Writings – Volume 1' which was published at the end of 2018.

'Collected Writings – Volume 2' was published at the end of 2019.

Ian now lives in Devon where he writes on a full-time basis.

Ian has several other writing projects in hand. You can follow the progress of these at **www.ianriddle.co.uk**

# *Also by Ian Riddle*

http://viewauthor.at/RIDDLE

*Available worldwide from*
*Amazon and all good bookstores*

---

www.mtp.agency

www.facebook.com/mtp.agency

@mtp_agency